Silver Brumby Kingdom

For Honor and John

Dragon
Grafton Books
A Division of the Collins Publishing Group
8 Grafton Street, London W1X 3LA

Published by Dragon Books 1968
Reprinted 1973, 1975, 1976, 1977, 1979, 1982, 1986

First published in Great Britain by
Hutchinson & Co Ltd 1966

Copyright © Elyne Mitchell 1966

ISBN 0-583-30070-7

Printed and bound in Great Britain by
Collins, Glasgow

Set in Plantin

ELYNE MITCHELL

Silver Brumby Kingdom

Cover Illustration by Peter Archer
Text Illustrations by Annette Macarthur-Onslow

DRAGON
GRAFTON BOOKS
A Division of the Collins Publishing Group

LONDON GLASGOW
TORONTO SYDNEY AUCKLAND

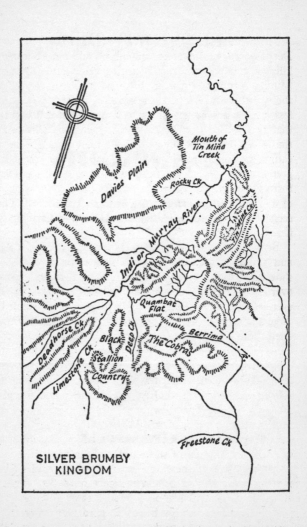

Mouth of
Tin Mine
Creek

Davies Plain

Rocky Ck

Indi or Murray River

Tin Mine Ck

Quambat
Flat

Berrima

Deadhorse Ck

Black

Deep Ck

The Cobras

Limestone Ck

Stallion
Country

Freestone Ck

**SILVER BRUMBY
KINGDOM**

One

Deep snow lay all over the mountains and on the lower foot-
hills for many weeks, so that spring came late. Down on the
Murray River the wattles bloomed close to the glittering
snow, but the grass and low-growing bushes were still lifeless and there was not much food for the animals and birds
that had come down out of the higher mountains to escape
the heavy winter. Grey thrushes flitted through the bush,
eating any food they could find; gang-gangs cracked what
gumnuts were left on the trees; most of the kangaroos hopped
further and further down the river, nibbling, browsing; some
of the brumbies, like Baringa, silver grandson of Thowra,
seemed to draw strength from the air and the sunshine, or the
fierce wind of the blizzards.

Benni, the little silver-grey kangaroo, friend to Baringa
and all the silver horses, sneezed as a warm gust of wind
showered his coat with the wattles' golden fluff, and he hopped
over towards Baringa. It had been the heaviest winter he had
ever known, and now something in this hot wind worried him,
though it should mean that spring was coming. Baringa, he
knew, had felt the coming of spring for days – felt strong and
full of vigour.

At that moment Baringa was enjoying the warm wind on
his coat and wishing that the snow had gone and that he was
able to take his mares to Quambat Flat, to gallop and play on
that great, open space, without fear of them being stolen
from him by his own dam's brother, Lightning, who grazed
there. Lightning was a silver stallion, like himself, but one
year older.

Anyway, feet of snow still lay everywhere, and Lightning
and his mares should be somewhere a good deal further up
the river, striving to live on a small area of grass and on the
tops of the bushes, just like he and his herd were doing.

Rumours had often come, carried by the birds or wandering kangaroos, of half a herd of beautiful mares who were

grazing even higher up the river than Lightning, and parted from their stallion by snow. Baringa thought of them now, while he was thinking of Lightning.

The warmth made Baringa sleepy, but he noticed again how the wind was making the snow melt, and that water was running down every slope. Perhaps the snow would go soon. It would be good to be racing and playing with Dawn and Moon, his two white mares, at Quambat Flat. His own Canyon, which hid them all so well, higher up in the mountains, was a good place, but he longed to have space. Now, as spring was coming, and he was a three-year-old, there was really no horse of whom Baringa was afraid. In the next two years he would grow stronger still, but already he had greater strength and resilience than any of the stallions he had seen – and far greater agility. Of Lightning he had some fear, because Lightning wanted his white and silver Dawn – would want Moon, when he saw her – and Baringa did not wish to have to fight and beat his dam's full brother, the son of Thowra.

He flexed his muscles, standing there by the gold-glittering snow, and dreamt of galloping at Quambat, but it was no good standing in the sun, dreaming. He would go up the river to see what Lightning was doing. He had stayed in the one place so long, and now everything was telling him that the time was coming to gallop and play, see new country, see new horses. He would go! And he went with springing strides. A few miles through melting snow, over soggy, wet ground, over rocks, round steep crags, and he would see the other horses: perhaps he would go round them quietly and see if the beautiful mares further up the river were just a story that the birds cried aloud.

Night fell before he reached Lightning's grazing ground, and he slept under some thick wattles, then moved on at the first light. Travelling was slow because there was much more snow than bare ground, and this was the second day of the warm wind so the snow was becoming very soft, as though there were no bottom to it. From a ridge, he looked out through the leaves on to the place where Lightning and his mares had been grazing when he last saw them. The mares were there, but there was no sign of Lightning. Baringa took a good look around. Yes, all the mares were there – the sweet, red roan. Goonda, whom Lightning had fought for

6

and won, way up on Stockwhip Gap, and her foal, and the pale grey mares he had won from a big iron-grey stallion, Steel. Lightning's tracks could be seen on the snow, going up the valley. Perhaps he, too, had gone to see if those beautiful mares were there. Baringa moved quietly away from the edge of the trees, and went on upstream.

In places he had to go through very thick snow. It was impossible not to leave almost a ploughed track, the snow was so soft, but he tried to keep among trees so that the track would not be seen from afar. It was heavy going, but it must be heavy going for Lightning too, and it was fun to be wandering about again.

Lightning must have got a start very early in the morning, because Baringa had been travelling for some time before he caught a glimpse of him. Knowing that he, himself, had grown, was stronger and felt ready to leap and gallop with joy – in spite of very little food throughout the winter – Baringa was anxious to get a good look at Lightning to see how much he had changed. It was so important that Lightning should realise that he could no longer steal Baringa's mares . . .

Lightning did not appear to have grown very much. If anything, he looked a little more set, but he was indeed a very handsome horse.

Baringa lost sight of him then, as they climbed yet another ridge. Beyond this there was a wide, splaying-out spur, turned to the sun, and bare of snow. Here five mares grazed. Baringa saw them, their colour, shape, age, in one quick, excited glance, and then looked round for Lightning.

Lightning was standing out in clear country gazing at the mares. Baringa watched him saunter down a rock rib that was free of snow and on which he could move easily, showing off his beauty.

The mares were all good looking, but two blue roans were outstanding. They were well built, with fine legs, and as they heard Lightning coming and threw up their heads to look at him, Baringa could tell that they were gay and spirited. He wondered what was going to happen. Their own stallion must have been away a long time. Did they think that he was gone for ever? Were they glad to see another stallion? Was he a nasty brute for whom they had no affection?

7

Was he, perhaps, handsome and spirited too, so that they would remember him for always, and resist any other horse's efforts to take them?

Baringa's ears pricked and he watched.

What did Lightning look like to those mares?

Lightning stopped, reared and called. To any mares he would have looked exciting. The five stood in absolute silence and not one moved, except for the flickering of their ears which Baringa could just see because they were outlined against snow.

Lightning dropped to his four feet and went closer, stepping high and cavorting, neck arched and tail held up to catch the sunlight and to ripple in the wind. The mares still stood without moving. Lightning got closer and closer to them. Baringa could see that he had picked the two best looking. Presently he was extending his nose first to one and then the other. The mares neither welcomed nor repulsed him. It was as though they were trying to size him up.

Lightning drew near to one and she suddenly snapped at him. He moved over to the other, and she kicked.

Baringa thought neither of them really meant it, and he wondered how far away the other stallion was. Even if he were quite some distance off, provided he had survived the winter, he must soon be able to get about because the snow was certainly thawing in this hot wind. Then he heard a kurrawong cry:

"Trouble! Trouble!"

Yes, there could be trouble if Lightning stole these mares – and it looked to Baringa as if the mares probably thought Lightning a very fine horse. He watched. He soon became certain, even from where he stood, that the biting and kicking was only half-hearted; and, by the way the other mares gathered closer, he guessed they would have liked to be chosen too.

Lightning began edging the two mares away from the others. Now they seemed more afraid, and the other mares kept closing in around them.

"All or nothing," thought Baringa. Now what would Lightning do?

8

Six kurrawongs came over, circled round, and began to cry:

"Trouble, trouble."

At least the kurrawongs were certain that the stallion was still alive and would come seeking his mares when the snow went. With this hot wind, the snow would go soon, even all this snow. Baringa looked at the hill-tops opposite, and they glittered white-gold in the sun.

Lightning now tried charm and blandishments, but when he walked away, all five mares followed him. He would have to take the lot, Baringa thought. Anyway, they were not bad lookers.

Lightning must have felt that five were too many. He tried to chase the others back, but after all it was not possible really to be nasty to three pretty little mares ... And the five stuck close together, so he succeeded in chasing them all. That was no good. Lightning stopped and called, not an imperious call, but a gentle one.

The five mares stopped. He called again. They half-turned, then they turned right round ... and all followed him.

"They are his!" thought Baringa. "All of them. Those mares have stuck out the winter together, and they're not going to be parted!" Baringa's eyes were gleaming with amusement as he went down off the hill and headed back for his own little herd which contained the two most beautiful mares in the mountains – Dawn, whom Lightning had wanted from the moment he saw her dancing in the spiral of silver mist on Quambat Flat, nearly two years ago, and Moon, her half-sister, still more of a dream than a reality to Lightning because he had only seen her clearly once, when she was running with a mad bay stallion, the Ugly One. Moon, then, had been only a half-believed dream to the horses of the south – the Hidden Filly – perhaps never seen, but now Baringa owned her.

A horse that owns the most beautiful mares in the mountains must either keep them hidden or be so splendid and strong himself that none can take them. Baringa knew this. He could hide them still, in his Canyon, below the High Plateau, but the time had come for him to roam wide and free, and there was only the thought of Lightning stopping him – Lightning whom he must not fight. Lightning for whom he still felt great affection.

The snow had become even softer, and the shine had gone from it. The heat was oppressive. For one moment Baringa wondered what was going to happen, but he was too taken up with his thoughts of the future and also of all he had just seen. He ploughed on through the deep slush. If Lightning saw his tracks they would not be recognisable. Perhaps he might get a fright thinking they had been made by the other stallion coming to find his mares!

The kurrawongs flew over again. "Trouble! Trouble!" sounded in their cry: "For theft there is trouble."

Two

The wind blew stronger, hotter, as the following day wore on, and neither Baringa nor his mares, nor Benni and his mate, Silky, knew why they felt that they should be moving upwards.

Evening came. The wind was still blowing, and, instead of cold air closing down on them, the night was hot. All the next day the wind blew, and all the next night. More and more water ran down the hillsides from the fringes of the snow. Once Baringa pawed at a thick patch of snow and found that it was rotten through and through. It crumbled and broke, then began to melt and join the little streams, the slowly moving sheets of water and the squelching swamps.

The horses and the kangaroos moved about restlessly, grazing here and there, filled with a dread they did not understand, and unable to obey their instincts and make upwards, because above them, everywhere, the snow was deep and now it was rotten, so that they could not get far through it at all. Baringa tried to force a way up once, the need to be higher was so urgent in his veins and his nerves, but soon found he was floundering, belly-deep, in glutinous, wet snow, through which he could no longer push his way. With every hour, of course, the snow retreated up the hill-sides, slithered off the rocks, broke and slid, became water; but even though, with every hour, they could walk higher on wet ground and pressed down

10

grass, the animals began to feel desperately that they should be higher, yet higher.

By the afternoon of the fourth windy day, heavy black clouds were moving over the sky.

It was Benni who, with his great wisdom, knew it first.

"We can't get high up the hillsides here," he said. "We must go further up the river."

"Even if Lightning sees Dawn and Moon?" Baringa asked, but he answered his own question by calling his mares and starting upstream. With them was Koora, a lovely, pale strawberry-roan mare owned by Thowra, and Dilkara, her foal, now nearly a yearling.

Benni wondered if they might get as far as Lightning. The river became narrower above where they had been grazing around the mouth of the Tin Mine Creek. Perhaps if they crossed the river . . . but it was already too late, at least for him and for Silky. The river was high.

"Baringa," he said. "Your mares might be safer on the other side. Over there, the country up above is not so steep."

Baringa looked at the water.

"Even now it is very deep and flowing fast," he said, and he looked at Benni, whom he loved dearly. "We will stay with you and Silky."

Night would fall soon, and it would come quickly because the world was already dark with cloud. The horses and the kangaroos kept on, scrambling along the rugged, steep sides of the river. Often they were held up by crags which were difficult to get round.

Baringa had been up the river three times since they were forced to come down the Tin Mine Creek from his Canyon during the winter. Once he went with Thowra and Storm, Thowra's half-brother, who had also been forced down this way from the Cascades when the very heavy snow fell, and who set off to work their way south and through the mountains, back to their herds. A second time Baringa went up the river merely to see if Lightning was still there – not to talk to him, because he had no wish for Lightning to know where he was wintering, or where he had his mares – and the third time was only a few days ago. Even if he had been over this country quite often enough to know it, it seemed strange and unfriendly in the hot wind and the gloom, and with the ominous sound of rushing water all around.

Rocks and earth were slippery with melting snow and water, and sometimes they had to plough their way through deep, rotten snow. It was a bad journey, and Dawn could not travel fast because she was very heavy with foal. Even Moon, whose foal would not be born till after Dawn's, found it hard going. The mares were anxious, too, for mares in foal or with young at foot are peculiarly sensitive to danger.

Each one, perhaps even the young colt, Dilkara, knew that it was water of which they were afraid, great water caused by the melting of the snow in the wind. They knew, too, that rain must be coming, but not even Benni could imagine what was going to happen, because snow as deep as this last winter's had never been in his experience, nor four days of constantly blowing hot wind on snow, followed by rain.

It was the instinct of the wild animals that told them all that here, in this narrow valley, with steep, high mountains on one side of them and the rushing river on the other, they were in great danger.

The rain started to fall – heavy, splashing drops of rain on their backs, on their ears. It made the going even more difficult, and made each animal more afraid.

Almost as soon as the rain started, the sound of the river grew louder, and the water through which they walked on the steep hillside grew deeper.

Then the rain began to pour from the sky so that the horses seemed to be pushing their way through a wall of raindrops, and the roar of wind, and rain, and water, began to sound in the hills all round them. They plodded on and on, still unable to climb upwards through the mushy snow on the precipitous hillsides. Once they tried climbing, and Moon slipped and fell, sliding fast in the mixture of snow and water on the shale surface. She gave a whinny of fear, but stopped sliding well above the river, and got shakily to her feet. Baringa and the others came down to her and, instead of trying to get higher again, kept on a lower level route, still going up the valley. And always the rain fell in unceasing curtains of beating, heavy drops: always the noise of the storm and running water increased.

12

A small flat where Baringa had grazed with Storm and Thowra was under water. The waters were gathering, rising and rising, and because they had never seen anything like this, and were still some distance from any place where they could climb to safety, the horses were becoming desperate.

Benni and Silky looked about them with their little anxious, pointed faces, trying to see somewhere to which they might go.

They passed a band of rock, difficult to climb over and round, and the footholds were not apparent in the gathering dusk and with the water pouring over the rocks. On the other side of it the river was far higher, half-dammed by the rocks, booming, coming up, up, up, rising faster than any of the animals had seen water rise before in ordinary springs. The river had a black, oily look as it rushed past.

Ahead of them, their way lay along cliff sides for several hundred yards.

"Get across here, and then we can work upwards," said Benni, but to get across the cliffs, with their slithering, sliding snow and pouring water, and all the time the rain beating down, was going to be very difficult.

"You lead," Benni said, "and I will come at the back, making sure that they all get over."

Dawn, looking frightened and tired, followed behind Baringa.

The cliffs did not seem the same as when Baringa had crossed them before. The water that rushed down them made them appear to move in the gloom, made each foothold precarious. Baringa picked his way with great care, becoming more and more nervous as he heard Dawn's short gasps for breath behind him, her occasional little half-whinnies of fear when her feet slipped and she fought to regain balance for her heavy body. And the river was roaring, rising, roaring.

There were only a few yards to go and then a fanning out of less steep ridge. Baringa looked behind. They were all still coming along, his line of mares, the foal and the two kangaroos. They had travelled like this, strung out across cliffs, three months before, but then it was through a curtain of falling snow that he saw them. Now it was this solid grey rain and oncoming night. One foot after another he picked his way on the wet, slippery rock.

13

There was a wild neigh and the scrabbling of hooves. He swung round, nearly falling himself. Dawn was over and sliding fast towards the swollen stream, desperately trying to right herself. He bounded down after her, neighing, with no thought of how he would stop himself. Even as he went, he heard a bark from Benni, but it was too late to answer – or to stop.

He had almost reached Dawn as she slid into the water. He saw her forefeet grabbing at the rocks: then she was rolled over and borne away by the fast-moving water.

Somehow, on small, wet toe-holds, Baringa managed to stop himself just at the edge, just before he, too, went in. He gave one anguished call, and then went leaping back the way they had come, though lower, near to that black swirling water, trying to race Dawn, trying to get down to some place where he might call her out on to flatter ground.

Below that narrow place of rocks, the river was not quite as fast; but what would happen to Dawn at the rocks? Clattering, crashing, splashing over precipitous stones and through water he went, looking towards Dawn's head which showed white, strained up out of the dark river.

When the river narrowed into the little rocky gorge, Dawn was near the furthest bank and swept up against the rocks.

Now, surely she would be able to get her feet down and fight her way out. Baringa watched her apparently feeling for something on which to stand, but the force of the water pinned her to the rocks and seemed almost to be building up against her, submerging her. She gave a despairing cry, and seemed to push off into the middle of the stream. There the water caught her and whirled her down between the rocks, out of Baringa's sight – and he had the rocky bluff to climb and get round.

Gasping, because all his breath had gone, he scrambled up and over, his eyes seeking the river on the other side of the rock barrier.

There was no sign of Dawn. Yes! Perhaps that was she, in midstream, being rushed along with the current – perhaps it was a white head in the darkness. Baringa galloped as best he could on the steep hillside, calling her. Then night came. There was one startling last cry from the kurrawongs somewhere in the sky.

Baringa could no longer see Dawn from the bank, and he sprang into the ice-cold river, swimming strongly down the stream. The cold was fierce, binding with steel bands, binding lungs and heart so that his breath became laboured and his movements weaker. How could Dawn survive in this? He was crashed into a rock, bruising his knees. He bumped his shoulder on another. He raised his head and tried to call, and his neigh sounded strange in the roar of the stream. There was no answer.

The dark, freezing water and the rain on his head were all that he could see or feel – a world of dark water and terrible cold, and the pain of the cold aching in neck, shoulders, ribs, quarters and all down the less protected bone and muscle of his legs, the pain of freezing. He swam on and on, his longing to find Dawn greater even than the deep instinct that was telling him to get to the shore, to get out, to save himself.

At last that instinct told him that, if he were to live, he must indeed get out, because he was so frozen by the snow-water that he was barely able to move.

The current had hitherto taken him down the centre of the stream, but now it started to whirl him towards the western bank. Baringa began to feel afraid, and wonder if he could find strength to swim across. He must get out on the eastern bank,

15

so that he could get back to Benni and the mares. Now even the pain of the cold was dying down. It was fear that suddenly made him struggle to swim, fear and a sudden tremendous determination.

For quite a distance the current bore him racing on, as though he, a huge silver stallion, were no more than a dry gumleaf, but slowly his efforts got him towards the other side. He felt rock under his hooves, he plunged towards the bank, fell, felt rock again and leapt. This time the bank was flatter and he dragged himself out of the current, on to the ground and into the lashing rain.

His great gasps for breath hurt his chest. He could barely move. Then, as he began to grow a little warmer, there was a different sort of pain all over: but there was no time to stop. Baringa started his weary struggle back to the others, splashing through the streaming water that came down from the snow above.

He took as careful note as was possible, in the darkness and the sheets of rain, of where he had pulled himself out of the river. He would have to get back, when daylight came, try to see Dawn, try to cross, try to get her back. On and on he went, trotting where he could, scrambling over rocks, slipping in the water.

Gradually the pain turned to a sort of tingling, and then he began to feel warmth again . . . and exhaustion.

He had to go very slowly over those cliffs where Dawn had fallen, so much water poured down them now that they were like an immense waterfall. When he came to the end of them, he threw up his head and called. Moon would surely answer him. He might even hear Benni's bark. He wanted desperately the comfort of being back with Moon, Koora and Benni . . . wanted their company because he so deeply wanted Dawn. Dawn meant more to him than any other mare ever would. She had run with him even when he was a yearling. She had refused to leave him and go with Lightning, who was already a handsome stallion when he was still a nervous colt. Dawn and he belonged to each other, and now she was gone. He called and then he listened.

An answering neigh, Moon's he knew, came from up above and a little further on. Presently he was walking on squelching ground instead of rock. He called again, heard the answer, and turned upwards.

Terribly tired, and more miserable than he had ever been, Baringa joined the waiting animals.

They had heard only the one set of hooves squelching through the mud, and knew he had not brought Dawn. Soft noses touched his nose, and Benni's gentle paw patted him.

"What happened?" Benni asked.

"I do not know," said Baringa. "I thought she went through that narrow gorge of rock. I could not really be sure I saw her head above the water on the other side of it, but I thought I did, and then darkness closed right down, and I went into the river to try to find her. I was swimming for so long, so very long, but I never found her." His head drooped down to the kangaroo, and the little soft paw touched his nose again.

"You got out," said Benni. "I think she will. Dawn has great courage." But he thought of Dawn and her foal so soon to be born, and he thought of the intense cold of the melting snow in the water.

"As soon as it is light, I will go back," said Baringa. "Are you and the mares safe here?"

"Wait and see what morning brings," Benni answered. "Here there is no food. We could not stay long, but I do not think the water will touch us."

Baringa listened, then, to the roar of the river, and if he listened carefully he could also hear, closer than the river, the strange, sibilant rustle of the water moving over every hillside as the snow melted. There was also the sound of rain.

Though the night was warm, he felt cold. He had been too frozen, he was also deeply tired, and he had lost Dawn. He went into a sort of troubled doze, standing there between the two mares, but he felt, all through the hours of darkness, that he was battling in the icy stream.

As daylight came, they could see the river was far, far higher than the night before, and so fast that logs and branches were hurtling down.

Baringa looked at it, feeling that he would have no chance in water that went at that pace, but he knew he must try to find Dawn. He looked round at the place they had spent the night. It was certainly the safest place he could see, but Benni was right: there was no food. It was a grass slope between rock outcrops and cliffs, and all the grass had been under snow until last night and was pressed into the mud. They would be quite safe there for a day or so, particularly as the sky, grey and misty, looked as if it would fine up.

"You cannot try to cross that river today," Benni said. "Wait. It will drop, probably by tomorrow."

"I think I could cross it, if I saw her," Baringa answered. "I must go down." And Benni knew he must.

The little herd stood dejectedly as Baringa left them, and they watched him start again over the streaming cliffs. He soon vanished from sight, and they had nothing at all to do but wait, and watch what went down the river. After an hour or so, the sun began to come through the mist and warm the air ... the sun that would also make the grass grow, though not today, and today they were hungry.

Baringa was below the rock gorge when the sunlight began to break through and fall in shafts into the opposite bank. If a silver mare stood in the bush, perhaps the light would gleam on hide or hair? He walked slowly, his eyes on the other side. He came to the place where he had dragged himself out of water the night before, and where, now, the river was much wider and deeper, and still he had seen nothing. He looked at the water, the brown, swirling water, and saw the back of a dead wombat being swept down. He hated the look of that river. He walked on downstream for a while, still staring across the river, and he still saw nothing. He called, but he did not know whether, standing so close to the roar of the water, he would ever hear an answer. He went back to the place where he had got out of the stream last night, then remembered that, just above it, there was a stretch of the river where the current swept towards the other side. He went a little further upstream, stood and looked for a while, at the great power of the steam, gave one more call, and plunged in.

He was immediately gripped by the iron cold, seized and twisted by a far stronger, faster current than he had dreamt possible. His chest crashed into a boulder. The water dammed up behind him for just one second, then poured over him, spun him, rolled him. He was past the boulder, legs bruised, water going into his ears, up his nose, tugging at mane and tail.

18

At last he came up, gasping for air, but the iron bands of cold around him made breathing almost impossible. Then a log hit his head and he swung round. His legs were among rocks, being twisted again, and the cold, the iron cold, froze him. He was swimming wildly, more to keep afloat than anything, but he saw that the current was indeed carrying him towards the further shore. How easy it would be to get out, he did not know.

Soon he saw that he was going to be swept against some rocks and then probably swirled out into the stream again. He struggled harder, trying to reach the bank upstream from the rocks. He felt his feet on boulders again, he tried to press himself on to them and make his way to the bank. Each time he slipped, he went further down in the current. Slowly, slowly he got closer to the edge of the flood. There was grass underfoot, he might make it. But every second he was also getting nearer to the rocks. Once he was swept against those, he would have no hope of getting out. He dug in his hooves and struggled at an angle across the current. His forefeet were on higher ground, his quarters were being swept away. With a prodigious effort, he got himself into shallow water and then leapt away from the river as though it might rise still further and catch him. He was weak and trembling.

It was time to start his search. He moved into the bush, wondering where to go. He called once and then listened, but the sounds he heard, blending with the roar of the flood, were only those of the birds. He searched the ground for tracks, and the only tracks were made by wombats or kangaroos. He turned downstream and walked on, searching and calling. Everywhere a great deal of snow had gone, and, in the warm sun, there was already the feeling of upthrusting life. This feeling, for all his misery, communicated itself to Baringa . . . but there was neither sign nor sound of Dawn.

Perhaps she had gone upstream. He turned back, moved further away from the river, and searched all the way back. When he was level with where he had crossed he went over to the river and continued upstream within the first thick cover of the bush. Not only could he see no trace of Dawn, but he was certain that no other horse had passed that way since the rain.

He went on and on till he felt he must be nearly opposite where he had left the kangaroos with Moon, Koora and Dilkara. He went to the water's edge and looked across, presently he saw them, way up above the water. He turned back into the bush and went on up the river. Not only did he still hope to find Dawn, but he had to get across somewhere where the water was not so high. Several times there were creeks to cross, each one swelled far beyond its normal size. In terror of being swept into the river, he went as far up every creek as the snow would allow, before trying to cross.

The sun had come out quite strongly, and he was hot. If the night were clear and frosty the melting snow would freeze again, and the water be stilled a little. He trotted on and he trotted hither and thither, eyes seeking track, nose seeking scent, ears listening for a call, but always there was nothing. The sun was sinking before Baringa was far enough up the river – to be able safely to cross. He was just below Lightning's grazing place and was amazed how much snow had gone from there.

Even that crossing was a struggle, and cold and bedraggled he turned back towards the herd.

Could it be possible for Dawn to be there when he arrived back in the half-light of evening? But it was Koora who extended her nose to his, Moon who rubbed against him, Benni who gave him a little pat.

"Tomorrow we will have to find a better place," said Benni gently, "somewhere where there is a little food to eat. I think there will be a few nights of frost, with less flood-water, but after that more rain may come."

Baringa shivered. He must find Dawn before rain started falling again.

Three

Baringa had noticed a better grazing place, not far up the river, where some of the bushes with leaves that were good to eat grew, so that even if the grass were dead and brown

20

from the snow, they would have food, and this place was well above the height of the flood-waters.

Next morning he took the kangaroos and Moon, Koora and Dilkara, and left them there while he went to cross the river higher up again, and to try once more to find Dawn.

There had not been a frost that night, and still more snow had gone off the hillsides. Baringa thought that it was quite likely that at least the banks of Quambat Creek might be bare . . . even possibly his own Canyon.

He decided to cross above Lightning's grazing place this time, so he would have to go high through the bush around it if he did not wish to be seen, and he was creeping carefully through flowering wattles when suddenly he realised that there was no one there. He went round it in case he had made any mistake, but the shrubby river point was empty. Then he came on the tracks, Lightning's tracks and the tracks of a number of mares. He followed them till he saw that they turned up Quambat Creek. So Lightning was going home, and, judging by the tracks, he was hurrying his mares along. Perhaps he had suddenly thought that the other stallion could now come looking for his roans, that most of the snow which held him back must be gone. Lightning was probably right, but what stupidity to leave such a clear trail!

Baringa crossed the Quambat Creek with some difficulty, and then went further up the Limestone before crossing it. It was very high, also he was wondering. . . .

Only patches of snow lay now where he had had to plough through it, following Lightning, not many days before. The hot wind and the rain had certainly melted it. He travelled quite quickly, even though he had to pick his steps very carefully so that he walked on stones, or rocks, or among thick bushes. He had a very strong feeling that the owner of the roan mares would be coming for them, and he did not particularly want his tracks to be found.

The sun was shining. It was hot and the wattles scented the air. Up here there was not the great roar of the flood, just a rushing song of water, and often the swish and slither of snow subsiding into a hollow underneath it.

Baringa did not take very long to reach the same hill from which he had watched Lightning steal the roan mares. As he climbed it, he could see that the opposite slopes no longer glittered with snow, though there were patches still – patches that could even look like a white mare sleeping. Then he was right on top, looking across and down, and ... He stopped, his coat pricking. ... There was something. ... He stood still amongst the snowgums, but his eyes moved over the whole of the opposite, splayed-out ridge and the one long finger of trees that came halfway down it. He must have seen a movement. *That* was not snow! Something white in the trees ... Dawn ... and it seemed as if he leapt, but actually he stood rock-still.

There was something in the trees. Stepping out of the leaves and the whippy, white branches, came a black stallion. Baringa barely breathed.

The stallion walked forward, head down, sniffing at the ground. The rain would have washed away scent and hoof-marks, but not all the droppings nor the pressed-down places where the mares had camped. Certainly it would be clear that several mares had lived here for months, perhaps clear that they were his own mares.

Baringa was thinking this and yet watching the trees, because he was sure something white had moved there. It could not be Dawn, but what was it? He watched, and out of the trees stepped a small, rather round, white mare.

This time Baringa did jump, but the stallion and mare did not see his movement. He forced himself to remain still but could not stop the sweat breaking out on his coat. It was not Dawn, but for one moment ...

In fact it was a good thing that the mare was not Dawn, because he could not bear to think of her having been even temporarily captured by another stallion, but he wished that he knew if she were alive and safe.

The black seemed to be getting more and more upset. He trotted everywhere, sniffing, and then would throw up his head and look all around. Once he called.

The white mare followed placidly, cutting corners, while the stallion's agitation drove him hither and thither.

Baringa watched carefully, so that he would know what that stallion had learned. He was sure there was no chance of Lightning's and the five mares' tracks down the river being still left to lead the stallion after them, and he was right. The black finally stopped rushing about and snuffling, and stood irresolute. He simply had no idea where they had gone.

If the black went down the river anyway, just because it was the easiest thing to do, Baringa knew that Lightning would be in trouble, because, down there, their tracks were so thick, and such a lot of them had obviously gone up the Quambat Creek.

The stallion, however, must have thought that if he stayed where his mares had wintered, they might return. Baringa could see that he had settled down to graze.

At last Baringa went off, crossed the Limestone, and began to search and search for Dawn.

Suddenly there was no sunlight. He looked up at the sky. Great, lazy grey clouds had rolled up and he had been so interested in the black stallion that he had never noticed them. Now he felt a quickening of anxiety. There would be more rain and the rivers would rise again. He must find Dawn. The weather was changing, quicker than even wise old Benni had expected. He must find Dawn. And soon he must take the mares back to the Canyon. He must find Dawn, he must find Dawn.

He searched the bush for her but he was terribly uneasy because of the black stallion. When he was opposite the place where he had left the mares and Benni, he went right to the edge of the swirling water and gazed across, trying to assure himself that they were all right. The bushes were thick, and for quite a long time he could see no movement at all. What if that stallion had come down the river, somehow not seen Lightning's tracks, and come right down here! But then he saw Benni peacefully grazing, and knew all was well. He went on with his search, desperately trying to find Dawn, but filled with fear for Moon and Koora, so that he knew he was not looking for her properly – though he had been over all this ground before – and knew, at the same time, that he was getting further from the others.

When he had gone quite a long way down the river and was opposite the mouth of the Tin Mine Creek, he could see that the Tin Mine, up which they might have to go to get to the Canyon, was probably bare of snow, and suddenly, definitely, he knew that he must take the mares and the kangaroos back there where they would be safe. He would go a little further down the river now, but though he trotted on, criss-crossing back and forth through the bush, it was so terrible to think he might lose Moon too, because he did not first take her to safety, that he worked himself into a frenzy.

He could not stand the anxiety any longer. He turned and went back, and once he had made up his mind to go, he travelled fast. In daylight, tomorrow, he would take them to the Canyon. Then, when he felt sure they were safe, he would come back and look for Dawn till he found her . . . if, indeed, she were there to find. Half of Baringa was sure that Dawn was so beautiful that she must be still living, and half of him knew that she may have been swept right down by the river, and drowned in the cold and the flood.

Driven by a nameless fear, he went faster and faster, so that he would still have plenty of daylight in which to see that black stallion and make sure he was still where he had last left him.

The black stallion was not there.

Baringa stood and stared. Even in his hurry up the river he had looked across to make sure that Moon was still safe, and had seen her with Koora, half-hidden in wattles, and there had been no sign of the black stallion then, so he did not really think that, while he was coming up the river, the black had gone down, though it was a gnawing possibility. Then he thought that if the horse had gone downstream he would most surely have found Lightning's and his herd's tracks, and followed them. Baringa had reached such a fever-pitch of anxiety during that day that it seemed everything could go wrong.

At last he began to feel certain that no horse was on the splayed-out ridge, and he moved quietly down through the trees. He should be able to pick up the black's tracks on the soft ground.

The tracks were everywhere. The black stallion had neat, strong hooves. The round, white mare had very small feet, they turned out slightly. Baringa was certain that she was not a daughter of Cloud, the great stallion of Quambat Flat, sire of Dawn and of Moon. He also thought that she might be sweet, perhaps not very clever, but sweet. He tried to unravel

24

the tracks, but they went everywhere, so then he turned downstream, but there were no tracks there, and he was very relieved. Eventually he found hoof marks leading up the Limestone, and since there was still daylight, and apparently no immediate danger to his herd, he followed.

The pair of tracks were perfectly clear on the wet earth. Baringa was as careful as possible to leave no mark. Occasionally, in boggy places, or where there were yards of bare, black earth, it was not possible, and then he stepped in the black's hoof mark. The black's stride was slightly shorter than his. It was also more indented than the mark which he made: the black was considerably heavier.

Baringa had to go rather further than he expected. After the black stallion's behaviour that morning – not knowing where to go – it would have been more natural for him just to wander. These tracks were purposeful. The stallion knew where he was going now – but why was he going upstream?

Darkness would come before Baringa got back to the others, he was going so far. However, he would be able to travel faster on the way back. Now he had to be cautious, since he did not want to burst out of the trees right on top of the black and his white mare.

He went on and on, and he was beginning to sweat. Any other time he would have been far more awake to the reason why he was sweating, but today he had become so desperate for Dawn, and he had been so afraid that something might happen to Moon while he was away, that he did not notice everything in the way he ordinarily did – such as the fact that it had got hotter towards the end of the day, when it should have got cooler.

He was trotting, now, through thick trees where he left no mark on the leaves and stones, and he was thinking about going to the Canyon and then spending days searching for Dawn – not thinking enough about what he was doing, when the trees ended, and he nearly went trotting out on to a pleasant grassy area. There, in the centre of it, beside a clump of snowgums, stood the black stallion and his round, white mare.

Baringa stopped just in time, thinking to himself that the black looked as if he owned the world, and then realising that this must be one of his usual camping grounds. He must have come back here, hoping the mares would come here too.

Baringa watched for a little while, sure that he was right, because both horse and mare seemed very much at home, then he turned to go back.

Just then the other reason why the black stallion had made upstream was brought sharply to his notice by a heavy drop of rain landing on his nose, then three fell on his back, and then it was raining in wide-spaced, big drops. He should have felt it getting hotter and hotter; he should have seen the clouds getting heavier and heavier.

The rivers would rise again, probably before he could get his herd to his secret Canyon. Once again he was filled with desperation.

He got down near the Limstone, where the water would soon wash away his tracks, and broke into a canter. He must get back to Moon as quickly as he could.

Four

Quambat Flat was only partly free of snow and there was very little to eat, but this was where Lightning and Goonda had grazed for two years, and they were glad to be back. The grey mares whom Lightning had won from Steel seemed to be pleased to be home too.

Lightning saw that Cloud, the grey stallion who had been chief of Quambat for years, was back too, with Mist, his mate, and his sister, Cirrus, whom Thowra owned. It did not matter that they were back first. Cloud must know that he, Lightning, was really the chief stallion of Quambat now, or he should know it, particularly now he could see this fine herd of mares.

Until there was more grass there would be almost too many mares! He had not meant to take all five of the roans, particularly as he had been planning to go over to the Ingegoodbee River to get a lovely chestnut mare whom he had not forgotten seeing when Thowra brought him and Baringa from the Secret Valley to Quambat Flat. This mare, he knew, was a direct throwback to Yarraman, her great-grandsire and Lightning's own grandsire – chestnut with flowing silver mane and tail, very handsome.

There was also, of course, Dawn, whom Lightning would dearly like to possess: and did Baringa have another white mare? He knew he had seen another white mare: where was she now?

It had been a muddy, slippery journey up the Quambat Creek, and they were all hungry. If the sun would continue to shine, grass must soon grow. Clouds were, in fact, already starting to come over.

Perhaps it would be good manners to greet Cloud and the two grey mares. Lightning left his herd near the chimney that stood as the one remaining sign of a hut which had once been there, and went up the flat, picking his way through patches of snow.

The great grey stallion greeted him and then rather anxiously asked for news of Baringa and Dawn since the heavy snow.

Lightning knew nothing except that Baringa had come like a ghost over the snow in the frost and the moonlight, and freed him and his mares from the pit of snow which they had unwittingly made for themselves.

"I do not know," he said. "I only saw him once during the winter. He came, a wisp of wind, over the frozen snow. He was well then."

Lightning did not much care to think of that terrible experience. He would know never again to let his herd stay huddled together in a close mob, stamping around, during a heavy snowfall, so that they allowed walls of snow to grow up around them. It was much more comfortable never to think of it, and never to think of how Baringa had led him back to Quambat through the black, burnt country, the summer before, when he was blinded by smoke. Not for a moment would he have admitted to himself that it was Baringa who always seemed to get him out of trouble. Baringa had even saved him once by distracting Steel – years ago, when Baringa was only a yearling and Lightning, himself, a two-year-old.

Cloud perhaps knew all this, and Cloud was sire of Dawn, the mare Baringa owned and Lightning wanted.

"It is going to rain again," said Cloud. "We will be safe. Here we are too high up in the mountains for any big flood."

The next rain will wash away nearly all the rest of the snow, Lightning thought, and then it would be possible to get over to the Ingegoodbee to look for that chestnut mare.

The first big drops fell while he was sauntering back to his mares. Those roans were certainly lovely, and here, at Quambat, there was plenty of room for a huge herd. More than likely the stallion who had owned them had perished in the snow.

He forgot the kurrawong's cry of "Trouble, trouble," and never even remembered it in the darkness of that rainy night, when he stood close to Goonda, under a candlebark tree.

The rain fell down all over the mountains, beating on the Main Range, washing the snow off Kosciusko into the Wilkinson Valley Creek and Cootapatamba Creek, washing the snow into the Crackenback River, into the Cascades Creek, into the Murray, into the Geehi, into the Ingegoodbee. This time the rivers were over their banks, high, deep and swift when it started, and the snow was even more ready to melt, so the waters rose and rose within an hour or so of the start of the rain.

The heightening of the river was already quite noticeable when Baringa was getting close to the place where he had left the others. He called, and they came into the open to meet him, all looking eagerly to see if he had Dawn, but so glad to welcome him back that he was heartened.

"No sign of her," he said before they could ask, because the emptiness of each day without her was terrible. He could not imagine that life should continue without Dawn, for she had never left him since that first day Thowra had taken him and Lightning to Quambat Flat.

"I must take you all back to our Canyon, so that I know you are safe," he went on, "and then I will search for her till I find her."

Benni turned his sad face away, and Moon rubbed against him because she could not bear to be left, and she could not bear him to be so hurt.

"It would be safer to wait till the rain stops and the rivers go down," Benni said at last, "unless we go up on the High

28

Plateau. I should think a lot of snow must have gone from there."

Baringa looked upwards, but night was settling down. Bare rock, bare earth and patches of snow all blended together into the dark and the heavy clouds and the rain.

"This is not a night for travelling over a steep mountainside which even you and I have never travelled before," said Benni. "Peace, Baringa. Sleep quietly here."

Baringa, who had gone miles and miles that day, but whose strength and energy were almost limitless, was still wide awake.

"I saw Lightning heading for Quambat," he said. "Goonda has become a beautiful mare. She is far more beautiful than the roans he stole. If the black horse comes . . ."

"Ah. It is a black?" Benni asked.

"Yes. I saw him today too. He could give Lightning plenty of trouble."

"Lightning has asked for it," Benni answered, but he was amused.

Before daybreak Baringa was already in a fever to move — but where? The rain was still pouring down, the river still rising.

"Perhaps," said Benni doubtfully, "we could get on to the High Plateau by going straight up above here. But wait, wait till the light comes."

A kurrawong called mournfully, somewhere in the just moving darkness.

"Tell me, Baringa," Benni went on, "have you looked for Dawn down this side of the river, beyond the Tim Mine Creek?"

"No," said Baringa. "I was so certain that she would have been taken to the other side by the current."

"You could try it — when you can cross the Tin Mine." He could look there, Benni was thinking, but how could a mare so soon to foal survive the force of that flood and the cold, the terrible cold?"

As the first grey light came, Baringa set off to see what was up above.

"I will not be long," he said, because he could not bear to leave them in case the black stallion came down the river, even

29

though it was unlikely while the rain still fell in sheets.

He would only go far enough to see what sort of climb was above them.

The clouds were so low, hanging over the edge of the High Plateau, that he could learn very little, but it looked as if they could climb it, and he was determined to get Moon away from any chance of being stolen by the black, also it was absolutely necessary to have her safely hidden away so that he could go seeking Dawn without any worry about Moon's safety.

The first part of the climb seemed quite easy. If there were cliffs above, he would find a way.

He went back and started them all upwards. Once they were on the move, haunches straining as they climbed, and rain spattering on steaming backs, Baringa felt better. He lost the look of dejection and went leaping up, eyes brighter, strength and gaiety in each spring. While he was moving, the future was his, even if the rain did pour down, matting mane and tail, making it constantly necessary to shake his ears.

Benni was thinking that if the gully up which they were climbing ended in cliffs, they might be in difficulty, because the ridges on either side were becoming very rocky. Baringa could already imagine them all safely in the Canyon, as though by magic he would surmount all difficulties. And in his mind's picture of them in the Canyon, there was also Dawn.

There were cliffs above, but Baringa and his herd were used to climbing. Once again he told them to wait till he found a way, and he scrambled up the narrowing gully and then went out on to the right-hand ridge of rock. Soon they would be at the top, then along the Plateau and down the other cliff, and then they would be in his Canyon – but there would not be Dawn. It was then, while he was imagining the journey almost finished, that he heard a "wumpf", felt a shiver go through the rocks under his hooves.

Then the rocks were moving.

For just one second there was no further sound . . . Baringa only felt the strange fluid feeling below his hooves as though a great current were taking the whole ridge. . . . One waiting second, and then the rocks started to rumble and there were the first crashes of stones falling against stone, and the whistle as they flew through the air.

30

Baringa leapt from a crumbling mass of rocks on to a huge boulder. He felt the boulder tipping over, canting into space, so that he was almost hanging in air before he managed to hurl himself off it, and then he was flying through space, righting himself, getting his hooves on to a rock, then, as it rolled to, twisting to jump once more, each time flinging himself a little further from the centre of the rock-fall. There was nothing firm on which to land. Rock-faces were folding, crumbling, foaming downwards: boulders were bounding past and Baringa was suddenly flying through the air upside down, trying to turn over, mane and tail caught by the wind, trying to get his legs underneath, somehow trying to save himself.

Down below, Benni and the mares had heard the first "wumpf" and the roaring of rocks, the clatter of stones. Then, through the mist and the rain, the stones began to pelt down.

Koora gave a wild neigh to call Dilkara, and leapt for the side of the gully and the left-hand ridge. Benni, usually so quiet, barked in horror. Each animal sprang away from the leaping wave of rocks.

Then through the air a silver horse was somersaulting. He was there and then he was hidden from sight, on the other side of the ridge, and it was impossible to get through the falling rocks to see what had happened to him.

As soon as the rock-fall had almost quietened, Benni went bounding through the last flying stones, across all the loose rubble and over the ridge till he saw Baringa picking his way rather slowly amongst the great scatter of rock. There were only some small splashes of blood blending with the rain on his coat, and though he walked slowly and kept shaking his head, he seemed all right. He was alive and he might not have been.

He raised his head, saw Benni and gave a low nicker. Benni hopped down to him and they touched each other, nose to nose – warm, trembling noses.

Benni watched him as they went on together. "He is not really hurt," he thought. "If he gets cold he will stiffen, but if he keeps going he should be all right." To Baringa he said: "Surely the other ridge would not fall too? We will have to go up that because this one may fall still more."

The other ridge, though steep and difficult, was at least solid.

31

At last the horses and the two kangaroos scrambled up into the wind and the lashing rain on top of the High Plateau.

Baringa, who was aching all over, turned thankfully towards the north-eastern end, towards the cliff above the Canyon. If he kept on now, he would get there, but if he stopped he might become too sore to move. The rain came down so hard that there was no need to worry about their tracks remaining. They skirted round patches of dirty, granular snow all patterned over with twigs and dead snowgum leaves, pitted with gumnuts. Even up here little runnels of water were everywhere.

When they reached the edge, Baringa and Benni peered anxiously over into the Canyon. If great flood-waters filled it they would have to stay up above, on the Plateau, in the roaring wind and the rain.

The creek was over its banks, but much of the flat was above water.

"It is too high to cross," said Benni with a sigh. "We will have to go back along the Plateau and into the creek much higher up." So wearily they went back along the Plateau and turned down into Dale's Creek, into the teatree, the silence, the loneliness and mystery of that valley.

They crossed the creek and got into the Canyon down the steep cliffs on its eastern side, hours later than when they had first looked into it.

There were the rocks and the trees they knew so well, under which they could shelter. There was a little food, and there was the sense of well-being and safety engendered by being in their own hidden place which Baringa had found when he and Dawn first ran together and needed somewhere secure to live, where the older stallions could not molest them.

That night Baringa needed comfort and security, for gradually he stiffened so that he could barely move.

For several days the rain poured down. At first Baringa grew stiffer and stiffer, then he began to loosen up, but his back was very sore where it had been twisted as the rocks threw him out into the air. He could not even walk easily. There was no possibility of him going to find Dawn till he could move more freely.

Benni went out one day after the rain had stopped. He hopped along up Dale's creek, then towards the track between

32

Quambat and the Tin Mine, to see if any one was about. It was there he saw Lightning – just leaving the track and starting towards Dale's Creek, nosing about as though he were looking for something. Benni watched for a while, then quietly headed back to the Canyon.

"Baringa," he said. "Lightning is nosing around in Dale's Creek. It might be a good thing if you went right round and came down from the Pilot towards him . . . if you can."

"I'll have to," Baringa answered. "I can move more now that it is a little warmer. Perhaps I will make my back better, if I trot about a little, and be able to go to look for Dawn tomorrow – if I make sure that there will be no trouble from Lightning, and see him safely home to Quambat."

Moving very stiffly still, Baringa climbed out of the Canyon and went along the ridge that divided Dale's Creek from the Tin Mine. He forced himself to trot along, and after he had been going for a while, though his back ached badly, no other horse just seeing him would have been able to tell that he had been hurt.

When he drew near to the Tin Mine-Quambat track, he went with the greatest care. He could see nothing, hear nothing. He examined the bare, wet earth of the track: Lightning had not passed there. With even greater care, he walked back towards Quambat Flat alongside the path till he came to where Lightning's tracks turned down towards Dale's Creek, then he looked and listened.

He could hear sounds from not very far 'away, rather as though Lightning were coming back to the track. Baringa went silently a little way up through the bush towards the Pilot, then, when he was sure Lightning was almost on the track again, he came down towards him, making just enough noise for Lightning to hear. Lightning must be certain to look up and see him coming down off the Pilot. If he could make Lightning think that he and Dawn lived in the silver forest of dead trees that was on top of the Pilot, so much the better.

Lightning looked up as Baringa carefully bumped one hoof against a log and let a branch break under another. Baringa saw him jump as though a fly had stung him.

Baringa walked a little further towards him and then he jumped, too, as if he had only just seen Lightning. It was

33

necessary to pretend that he had not seen him at all this spring, that he had not known whether he had survived the heavy winter or not.

The two silver stallions greeted each other with friendliness.

"Where are you going?" Baringa asked cheerfully.

"I thought I would go over to the Ingegoodbee, and try to find that lovely chestnut mare we saw when Thowra brought us through to the south," Lightning answered. "Why don't you come too?"

Baringa remembered the golden chestnut with silver mane and tail. Thowra had told him that she was a throw-back to her great-grandsire, Yarraman, for she was a daughter of Son of Storm, and Storm was Thowra's half-brother and great friend, both of them sired by Yarraman. Yarraman was Baringa's great-grandsire too.

"I will go with you," he answered, realising that was the only way in which he could know what Lightning was up to. "I have seen the mare some time ago, running in the herd of a chestnut who is *not* of the Yarraman line – rather plain. His bimble is under the Pilot, close to where the Tin Mine Creek heads."

"You seem to know," Lightning said, and his voice had a suspicious edge to it, his eyes a suspicious gleam. "Is the chestnut horse quite a fighter?"

"I don't know," Baringa replied carelessly.

"Well, let's go," said Lightning, setting off at a trot.

Baringa let him lead along the track, then he followed through the bush at one side, where his hooves would leave no mark and where his silver shape was not visible.

After a few minutes Lightning turned round suspiciously.

"Where are you?" he asked, his voice almost angry.

"Here," Baringa answered, poking his head through a bush.

Lightning snorted and went on.

Presently he swung round again. Before he could speak, Baringa stuck his head out from some hop scrub on the other side of the track.

"Why can't you get behind and follow me properly?"

"I'm coming, never fear," he said. "Keep going."

34

Lightning's temper was rather frayed by the time they reached the Tin Mine Creek.

"Now where to?" he asked Baringa, and he sounded sharp.

"Up the creek," said Baringa. "It might be better if you kept in the bush along here."

"I will go as I wish to go," answered Lightning. "I don't think there is a horse in the bush to beat me!"

"No?"

"Come on," said Lightning. "This is going to be fun."

There were great patches of snow all the way up, and often the track ran fetlock-deep with water from the melting snow. It was possible, Baringa could see, that much of the chestnut stallion's bimble around the head of the creek could still be under a huge drift. He wondered where the herd might be – but most herds would be making back to their own country now.

Lightning led on and on, right to the Tin Mine Creek, and then turned upwards. In places the valley was a sheet of water. It was all boggy, and the brown, lifeless grass was muddied. There was no grazing and there were no horses to be seen in all the wide, gentle valley which Baringa thought of as always green and fresh, and golden with daisies.

Somehow there should be horses about. He looked far and wide again – and nearly bogged.

He pulled each foreleg out, squelching, and stood for a moment, to ease the pain in his back. It would not do for another horse – or even Lightning – to know that he had been hurt and might not be able to fight as well as usual, nor gallop as fast. The slippery, wet ground had been bad enough, each slip had wrenched his back, but bogs were even worse.

Lightning went on. It was Baringa who saw the first hoof marks, but Lightning was heading in the right direction, so he kept quiet and just saw to it that he, himself, was even better hidden and left no track. Lightning was expecting fun – well, there could be fun if he burst on to a mob of horses unexpectedly.

Their way was blocked, after a while, by a broad drift of snow. Even there Lightning missed seeing the tracks which crossed the drift just above where he did. He was starting to get impatient, and had quickened his pace. The snow was solid and soon he broke into a canter.

Baringa went along more carefully, on the top tracks, fitting his hooves into the spoor of, he imagined, a tall mare. The stallion's hoof marks were too close together for comfortable movement. He noticed how wide-splayed his hooves were, not like the usual mountain breed. One was badly broken: probably he was a soft-hooved horse, could be bad-boned.

Lightning stopped, turned round to make sure Baringa was coming, and then started off smartly again. There was a thicker bank of trees ahead. Baringa, in spite of the pain in his back, hurried forward. He was sure he remembered something about this particular piece of country. He and Dawn had climbed up this way to the Pilot (if only his back would recover enough for him to get through the flooded river, he could go to find Dawn) and surely there was a hollow on the other side of the trees, a hollow that was usually filled with sweet grass? There was such depth of snow in the drift that it masked the fact that the belt of trees grew on a small ridge. Baringa got there only a little later than Lightning.

Lightning cantered through the trees, not worrying if the country ahead were clear or not. Baringa stopped, saw the herd ahead in the sweet grass hollow which was now a mixture of water, mud and snow, and then saw Lightning, unable to stop, sliding fast down a great bank of snow, sitting back on to his haunches, gathering speed, snow frothing up around him.

The herd simply stood and stared. There was the chestnut mare and the chestnut stallion: there were other mares.

Lightning slid faster and faster, and the stallion gathered himself together and rushed towards him. Baringa watched carefully from the trees. Lightning was going to be well off balance when he hit the bottom. He was on his side: he was rolling over: he was up!

The rather ungainly chestnut stallion looked as if he did not know what to do.

Some of the mares threw up their heads and tails, and galloped through the mud to the other side of the hollow, but the Yarraman mare stood still.

She was certainly handsome – golden and silver in the sunshine, and a bank of gold-lit snow behind her – but Baringa

36

could only think of two mares in all the mountains, Dawn and Moon.

Lightning regained his balance and his dignity, and walked straight up to the chestnut mare as though the stallion did not exist.

The stallion snorted with fury.

Lightning stretched his nose out to the mare. Baringa wondered if he were going to be silly enough to let the chestnut stallion get in the first blow, but suddenly Lightning whipped round to make a spring at the horse.

Unfortunately the ground was more than muddy, and Lightning's feet went from under him.

The chestnut was so surprised that he missed the opportunity of jumping on top of the fallen horse.

Lightning heaved himself up out of the mud. This time he moved more cautiously, but it was obvious to Baringa that the floor of the hollow was either bog or sheets of firmer ground which were as slippery as ice.

Lightning made a few cantering strides towards the other horse, tried to stop so that he could rise on his hind legs and strike, but simply went sliding on till he crashed into the chestnut's shoulder. This turned out to be an unexpectedly useful action, because it pushed the chestnut into a bog. Soon mud was flying everywhere, Baringa could barely see the two horses.

The chestnut's big, flat feet should be a help, he thought, and they were, because he did not sink as easily as Lightning did. For a moment or so the mud was only flying up about girth high, and Baringa could see them both, almost stuck fast, snaking their necks and trying to bite each other. The chestnut got his legs free first, struggled out on to firm ground, and landed a few blows on to Lightning's shoulders, but he was not much of a fighter, he backed away as soon as Lightning began to pull himself out of the bog. Then Lightning tried to chase him but his legs went slithering in every direction. The great, wide feet got a better grip, and the chestnut kept out of range. Lightning, following, was blinded by the churned-up mud.

Baringa had pushed himself right in among the arched-over branches of a bowed snowgum so that he would not be easily seen, but just then, as Lightning floundered into another bog hole, he noticed that the chestnut mare kept gazing at the trees in which he was hidden. Soon he was certain that, out of the puzzle of cream hide and cream bark, silver hair and silver bark, tracery of red-brown twig and black branch, and the over-all covering of olive-green leaves, she had pieced together the silver horse that was himself. He did not feel very worried about this. He could not realise that not one mare who had seen them, even as colts when they went south with Thowra, would ever forget them, nor would he realise that even then, when only a yearling, he was the most unforgettable of the two.

He watched the two horses floundering, slipping, sliding, falling, and rarely getting in either a blow or a bite. He hoped they were not just going to collapse of exhaustion. He was anxious to see Lightning at least started on his way home to Quambat, and his back was hurting.

The shadows were already growing long when, with some relief, he saw Lightning backing away from the chestnut, and the chestnut making no effort to follow him.

Baringa slid out quietly from among the branches. Lightning

38

started in surprise when he saw him there, having apparently forgotten everything except the fight and the mare.

"Come on. Let's get out of this," said Baringa.

"I want that mare," Lightning answered.

"I'd say that was up to her." Baringa's words had an edge to them. "You're neither of you – you or the chestnut stallion – worth an empty gumnut at the moment. I'm going. You'd better come, or you'll meet another horse when you are too exhausted to fight," and he began to move off into the trees, silently blending into the pattern of light and shade, trunk and branch, leaf and grass.

"Come!" Lightning called imperiously to the mare, and he followed Baringa. There was no movement from the chestnut stallion, who stood blowing and sweating.

The mare did not move either, but when they had been gone a few minutes, she too had gone.

As the sunset light flared and died, Baringa realised that one other had joined them. He looked back and saw her following. The three kept jogging on through the bush.

Darkness had closed in before they reached Quambat, but there was sufficient light from a great full moon for Lightning to see his herd of roans and go straight to Goonda.

Baringa vanished then, slid away to one side through leafy trunks that had been badly burnt the summer before – vanished so that even the chestnut mare, who would have followed him through fire and blizzard, never saw him go, though she knew almost immediately that he had gone.

Five

The full moon was now only a three-quarter moon shining down on Quambat Flat. For the second time the chestnut mare, Yarolala, had gone, and Lightning knew that she was searching for Baringa. He had been furious to find that she did not really wish to be his, that it was Baringa with whom she longed to run. Now she had gone again. Oh well, last time she failed to find him and she had come back to Quambat. She would come back this time.

He grazed quietly beside Goonda, who, as the grass started to grow, was becoming even lovelier than the stolen blue roans, but he could not stop restlessly wondering about Baringa. Baringa had more than one mare: who was the second one? Baringa had come down off the Pilot, but did he run there always? Where did that other white filly run, and why had no one heard of her since the big fire, last summer? Could Baringa own her now? This was a question that had been eating into Lightning ever since he came back to Quambat when the snow melted.

That unknown filly had looked so lovely, during the only fleeting moment in which he had seen her. She was just like Dawn, and Dawn was the most glorious mare he had ever seen.

What if Yarolala did not come back? *If anyone could find Baringa, she might.*

Yarolala's track was easy to pick up – easy even for Lightning – because she had jumped on a very sharp rock, two days ago, and made a triangular nick in her near fore hoof.

"I am going to find Yarolala," Lightning told Goonda, and, barely hearing Goonda's rather tart reply that Yarolala had no wish to be found by anyone but Baringa, he set off in the direction of the Pilot ridge.

He would have kept going that way if he had not suddenly got the fresh scent of Yarolala, and then seen her spoor on some bare earth, and he followed her on to the Tin Mine track. For a long way he trotted along unthinkingly, then her scent seemed to have vanished. He looked for her spoor, and it had gone.

Annoyed, Lightning turned back till he found it again – and found, to his surprise, that she had turned left, off the track, north and westward.

This was rough country, and it needed more than Lightning's cunning to follow her spoor over the stony forest floor and the patches of snowgrass, but he persisted, and, more by luck than skill, he found himself where her scent lingered and where a footmark told·that she had passed, just on the gap where Dale's Creek headed, on the north, and the Pilot Creek on the south.

Yarolala was going towards the north.

Lightning stopped and wondered. He had only once been any distance down Dale's Creek, and that was the day in which the whole bush had burst alight. He had seen the filly whom they called the Hidden Filly then, and had started to fight the stallion with whom she ran, the Ugly One, but the fire had come. There was, he knew, snowgrass nearly all the way down the creek, so that no hoof mark would show, and there was thick teatree which could hide Yarolala or hide another stallion.

He stood there, undecided whether to go on or not. The moon shadows were growing longer as the night passed. There was no sound of Yarolala, perhaps he should go home. He put his nose to the ground and sniffed. Her scent still lingered.

She was a strange mare, and lovely. She seemed to be one always to graze on her own, seeking no company – except Baringa's. He sniffed the scent of her again – strange and lovely – *and if anyone found Baringa, she would*.

Lightning began to move slowly down into the valley of Dale's Creek.

He walked past the hanging valley where Baringa had found him blinded by smoke and fire, not letting himself think of it. He walked slowly over the moon-blanched snowgrass, across the shadows, step by step, along Dale's Creek. A wind whispered, the shadows moved and wove together. He stepped nervously over them, through them, stepped nearer, nearer, nearer – nearer to what? Yarolala? Baringa? The filly who had once run there – charred bones and hide, or lovely shape of life?

On he walked down Dale's Creek, on and on, nearer, nearer.

After a while he realised that there had been no sign nor scent of Yarolala for at least a mile. He cast around, but there was not enough bare earth for a hoof print, and he could not find her scent. He wondered whether he should go back till he found trace of her again, or whether he should keep going. Feeling more and more doubtful, he kept on.

The moon shadows grew longer and they slowly paled as light filtered up the eastern sky. Lightning found himself going slower and slower. There was still nothing to say that Yarolala had come so far. He felt less and less inclined to go on. Perhaps she had already returned to Quambat.

He turned round to start back, felt sure there was someone
41

close to him, looked this way and that, and then saw her. She was just a shadow in the half-light of the moon and the day – Yarolala and no one else. But what were the things walking towards her, weird shadows of grass trees?

Lightning felt suddenly muddled, puzzled, twisted. Who was coming from which direction? What were those strange things that walked and trembled like the fronds of grass trees? Half-lit by the waning moon and the first creeping light of day, and here, near where he had found the Ugly One, the moving grass trees filled him with terror. He stood shaking, so frightened that he could almost feel himself galloping through the bush, anywhere, anywhere to get away. But Yarolala was there.

"Come, Yarolala, come!" he called, but it was as though she did not hear him.

He saw that she had turned to the moving bunches of fronds and was walking towards them. Then he saw, in that faint light, that they were not covered with fronds, but with feathers, and he saw the beaks, the immensely strong birds' legs and feet, and, as they got closer, the fierce, darting eyes. The emus!

Lightning should have remembered the emus. Once, when he was only a two-year-old, and being chased by Steel, they had called to him to go to Cloud for safety. They liked to be too wise, the emus, that was all.

Lightning's fears calmed down, but because he had been very frightened, he now became angry.

"You come back with me," he said to Yarolala, and walked towards her to give her a little nip and show her that he was master.

She was taking absolutely no notice of him, not even looking at him, but very respectfully saying to those queer-looking birds:

"Greetings, O noble birds," just as though she had been trained in manners by Thowra, "I know that there is no secret of the bush which you do not understand, and there is something I would very much like to ask you."

A pleased expression came over the two fierce and rather silly faces.

42

"Ask, O beautiful Yarolala. The secrets of the bush are indeed ours."

Lightning drew closer, so greatly interested that his anger sank.

"I would know," said Yarolala, who never dreamt that Lightning himself did not know, "where the silver stallion, Baringa, runs?"

Lightning came closer still, and the emus shot him a quick, fierce glance. They did not wish Yarolala to lose any of her belief in their wisdom, and must not let her, or Lightning, know that they simply had no idea where Baringa hid.

The male bird answered:

"That is a dangerous secret, Yarolala, too dangerous for one as gentle as you."

"I am not gentle," said Yarolala, and she spoke fiercely. "Do you know where Baringa runs?" Almost immediately she tried to cover her lapse from manners by adding: "I am sure you do, for what secrets are hidden from you?"

The emus had begun to flutter their feathers with annoyance, but her covering remark smoothed them down. The female emu looked sharply at her.

Yarolala pleaded:

"Wise and noble birds," she said, "please could you let me into just this one of your secrets."

"Perhaps we might lead you there in the dark of the night," the female bird said.

"No," said the male, "not yet. She would have to be wise enough to keep a secret. Come, it is time we walked on, if we are to graze at Quambat Flat during this day that is breaking now."

"I will not allow you to be at Quambat unless you tell me where Baringa hides," said Lightning.

Yarolala looked at him in surprise, but even then she was too taken up with her own wishes to realise that there might be enmity or jealousy between the silver stallions.

The emu sneered, and when he sneered he looked nasty.

"It is not for you to stop us," he said, and he and his mate strode off through the bush.

"Come!" said Lightning, and this time Yarolala followed him.

It was quite true. Lightning, unless he really savaged the emus – if he could – had no way of stopping them from visiting Quambat.

He was glad to be back at Quambat, glad to be with his mares. The day was warm and pleasant. Yarolala seemed to settle down quite happily, grazing in the sun, cantering round with the foals or other young mares.

"You are very fast," he said to her once.

"My name means 'to fly'," she answered proudly, and did a quick gallop round him.

She *could* go fast. Next time he noticed her, she was over near the emus.

The warm sun and good grass had made him sleepy, and one of the blue roans was telling him a tale of the far south and of a strange, lone stallion, a killer, whip-thin, nimble and fast ... He supposed that if Yarolala did find out where Baringa hid he would be able to follow her, but he really thought that those two over-wise birds would not tell her – or that they simply did not know.

It was Goonda who overheard the emu saying sharply to Yarolala:

"Stay with the stallion who wants you, and seek not Baringa. He has mares of his own who are the sun and the moon to him," for they had seen Baringa once with Dawn and Moon.

Goonda felt sorry for Yarolala, as she watched her walk away from the emus, then she looked across the flat at Lightning. She remembered that when Baringa freed Lightning and the mares from their yard of ice walls, Lightning had promised him to leave his mares alone. She looked at Lightning and she wondered if he would keep his promise. Goonda was fond of Baringa.

One lovely, peaceful, sunny day followed another: grass and leaves began to grow. Yarolala had apparently quietened down, then a cloudy night came, at the dark of the moon, and she was gone.

Lightning was very angry. None of his mares had noticed her go, though Goonda seemed uncomfortable about her and did not say much.

"I will go and find her," said Lightning, who thought she might have learnt of Baringa's hiding place from the emus.

44

"The emus told her not to seek Baringa," Goonda said, hoping to put him off, but Lightning went away into the night.

All the way up Pilot Creek, he got an occasional trace of Yarolala's scent, enough for him to know for certain that she had come this way, enough to keep him jogging purposefully along.

He reached the gap. There was a faint movement of wind in the trees, taking away scent. He dropped his nose to the ground. Yes, her scent still hung there. Then he went over the other side.

He was out of the wind soon, and almost immediately he realised there was no scent there. He went hither and thither to either side, but he found no trace of Yarolala. At last he went back to the gap. The wind had become stronger, and the most noticeable smell was that of bruised eucalypt leaves, but just once he knew he was on the track of Yarolala, going a little towards the Quambat Ridge – then there was absolutely nothing more.

Search though he did, he could pick up no trace of her. At last he went home, thinking she must have turned back, but she was not there. In the morning she did not return, nor did she come back in the afternoon.

Six

Baringa's back had improved enough for him to be able to climb up on to the High Plateau, and for him to be sure he could cross the river. It was the time of the dark nights when there was no moon.

He left the mares with Benni in the Canyon, and climbed up the cliff one night. This time he was not worried about them. Already there was a little grass to eat. Each day the sun was warmer and there was the feeling that the whole world was bursting into life – blade, leaf, flower, animal, insect and bird. On one sunny rock he had seen the purple splash of sarsaparilla: soon there would be more food than they could all eat.

In the Canyon, Moon would be safe, and Koora safe for

Thowra, when he came. Baringa knew he need not worry about them. This time he could search and search till he found Dawn.

He would go along the High Plateau and follow Quambat Ridge down to the river, go up the Limestone a little way before crossing, in case she had made her way upstream, then explore all the western bank of the river, far down it and even inland. However long it took him, however far he had to go, he would seek Dawn till he found her, and always, as he climbed the cliff and went along the High Plateau, it was as though Dawn were ahead, a white and silver ghost, so strongly did she fill his mind.

He went quite fast, and as he went the remaining pain in his back eased away. The night was warm. The scent of eucalypt leaves filled the air. No scent of horses was on the whole long ridge. He walked with pride, for he felt strong again, and to be alive in the soft spring darkness was high magnificence.

He also held himself in readiness for anything that might come out of the dark net of night.

As the ridge began to drop down to the river there was the fragrance of lightwood flowering. A mare neighed near by, as though she knew that the most wonderful stallion in all the southern mountains was going past in the thrilling night.

Soundless, Baringa moved on and on through the bush.

It was only chance that made Yarolala turn west from the gap between the head of Dale's Creek and the Pilot Creek. She had been down Dale's Creek before and found no tracks, nothing but those supercilious emus. She really had no fixed plan for where she would search, and she had no idea where Baringa might run. She might just as easily have turned towards the Pilot, but she turned west and upwards towards Quambat Ridge.

It was just chance, too, that she started her journeying much later in the night than Baringa did.

She climbed up on to the ridge.

If it had not been for a faint south wind starting up then,

Yarolala would have turned up on to the High Plateau, but on that south wind there came . . . something.

Yarolala stopped. Her nose trembled. She lifted her head to the breeze and drew it in, and a tingling went through her, right to her hooves and through every hair. Then she turned into the breeze – walked into it as though it held her – and the breeze that lifted her silver mane and forelock carried the scent of Baringa.

Yarolala kept on walking, head up to the wind, never losing that scent, even when the ridge dropped down in among the flowering lightwoods. She simply followed the scent as though she were led on an invisible string by the horse ahead, over on to the banks of the Limestone, along and along the track. Sometime he would stop to graze, then she would find him.

There was no sound of hoofbeat ahead, but Yarolala, of course, was not soundless. She could have been heard by any horse who was close enough, but not by Baringa, because the wind bore the sounds away.

The darkness before dawn grew heavier, then there seemed to be a faint movement through it. Yarolala felt, almost more than saw, a shiver of grey – and still there was the scent, drawing and drawing her.

Faint blue illumined the dark. The trees were thinning and the scent grew stronger. Yarolala slackened her pace. Baringa might have stopped. She felt less sure of herself. She walked more quietly.

As she came to the edge of the trees, she paused. Ahead were rocks, heaped up rocks and flat rocks looming through the strange half-darkness, and below them seemed to be empty space, probably a grassy glade, perhaps a small creek.

Just as she made out the shape of Baringa between two great rocks, she heard a sound behind her and knew that she, too, was being followed.

"Lightning!" she thought, and stepped swiftly to one side, amongst thick trees.

There was the scent of Baringa still, strong on the breeze, drawing her, and through the thick leaves she could still see him, shadowy and insubstantial because there was no light. Then something hurtled past her along the track, sprang on to the rocks, sprang on to Baringa.

47

Yarolala gave a little cry and then stood silent. Baringa had leapt forward so that the other horse only crashed down on to his rump. In the resulting mix up of two stallions, and in the blue, shadowy light, Yarolala could only just make out that the attacker was not silver, not Lightning.

Baringa's quick leap had saved him, but it had also put him in a difficult position for dealing with the other horse. He reared up and swung round in one move. The other horse was already coming in to attack. Yarolala had time to see that he was no horse that she had ever seen before, then there was an interlocked, moving mass of stallions as Baringa leaped upwards on his hindlegs and brought his forelegs smashing down on the advancing head and shoulders.

The horse roared with anger and tried to force him backwards over an edge of the rocks. Yarolala could hardly stop herself neighing a warning, but Baringa must have felt the air behind him and known that there was space. He stood firm. There was no room to jump to either side, so Baringa had to force himself against the terrific impact. The horse recoiled. Yarolala drew in her breath as she saw Baringa sway and then gather himself together enough to jump away from the edge.

In the bluish light, everything looked queerly fluid. The attacking horse seemed grey, the rocks were all caverns and hollows. Baringa faded into the atmosphere. The horse was leaping forward again. It twisted in the air, its teeth bared.

This was surely a very nimble horse, almost as nimble as Baringa, and it had the advantage of knowing the rocks in which they were fighting.

Then Yarolala saw Baringa leap on to a flat-topped rock above his opponent, obviously playing for time so that he could see the country over which he had to fight. She saw that other horse spring on to an opposite rock and fly across at Baringa, clearly knowing the distance between rock and rock so well that the queer quality of the ending night and the unstarted day did not make him falter.

Baringa had vanished. For a moment he was invisible in the strange light into which he had blended, but Yarolala saw him again, balanced on a sharp rock.

She looked closely at the other horse. Why had he attacked

48

Baringa? Who was he? She remembered the story that Lightning's stolen roan mares told of a lone horse, a killer. This could be close to the killer's country – and the roan's country. Perhaps this horse was the killer. She began to sweat with fear, not fear for herself, but for Baringa, who now, fighting, was even more unforgettable than before.

The two stallions were back on the flat rock now, locked together. They freed themselves, they were dodging each other's blows, they were leaping from rock to rock again. The blue light shimmered over them. Baringa seemed to be disembodied light itself, taking shape and then vanishing, becoming solid as he jumped or struck, then melting into the moving blue again. They were both so nimble that neither succeeded in sinking his teeth into the other, or in striking more than glancing blows as the other dodged.

Baringa stood quite still for a few seconds and merged so with the atmosphere and the rocks that "the killer", if it were really he, made a mistake, and came in too much to one side. Then Baringa, momentarily possessing the form of a horse in the blueness, gave him a tremendous blow on the head.

Yarolala watched Baringa streak forward to follow up his advantage with yet another crashing blow, but the other horse seemed less shaken by the hit on the head than one could have expected, and, as Baringa came through the blue air, he dodged out of the way and then back to attack.

There they were, dodging, leaping, rearing – a whirl of horse, and nothing taking substantial form in that moment before it was light. Then light came sliding over the sky, and there were two distinct horses fighting a strange fight that rarely brought them close enough to touch each other. Baringa's enemy was a chestnut. The roans had said the killer horse was chestnut, tall, rangy. This must be he, Yarolala thought. Bolder, they called him. He was a horse that wandered far and wide, they had said. Yarolala was trembling. Yes, this must be Bolder, and he did indeed look like a killer.

Baringa seemed lighter, she thought. He might be swifter too, but in nimbleness they were completely even.

Just then Baringa must have decided that these rocks, in which Bolder obviously knew every foothold, every crack, were no place to fight, because he took a wild leap through the gold-glittering air and landed on a little grassy flat below the rocks. Rocks and trees enclosed this flat, but on the grass Bolder would have no advantage. There Baringa waited for his attacker, his brave, yet gentle head thrown up, his silver mane glistening.

Bolder sprang after him, and they danced round and round each other in the snowgrass ring. While they fought on and on, neither doing much damage to the other, Yarolala moved down through the trees so that she could see them better.

"They will fight till they are exhausted and then fight again," she thought, but what would happen in the end? A horse was never given a name for being a killer for nothing. She wondered if Baringa were anxious, then she saw that he was enjoying the soft snowgrass underfoot. She watched him do several light springs.

Bolder came dancing in to strike him. Baringa stood his ground, then dodged at the last minute, got in a good kick at the chestnut's shoulder, and was out of reach again in a flash. Then Yarolala knew that Baringa had determined to attack, but that even the nimble chestnut could not guess how, or where.

Baringa darted here, there, everywhere. He circled fast around the other horse. Then he was coming in on the chestnut's forequarter, but like a snake, from side to side, and fast, so fast. His teeth had grabbed. They missed the hold for which he had aimed – on the wither – but they sank into Bolder's neck. For a few minutes the two horses were locked together, dancing and swaying in the sunlight. Yarolala saw Bolder getting himself ready for a mighty heave – Baringa must have felt it. Before he could be thrown off Baringa let go his grip, twisted on his haunches, and struck again at Bolder's head.

Once more they were dancing around and around each other. Baringa looked as though he were enjoying himself and also as though he could go on for hours.

They did go on and on. Yarolala crept off to get a drink in the middle of the morning. When she came back, the little, churned-up grassy flat was empty, and her heart gave a jolt inside her. Had she lost Baringa again, when, in a way, she had barely found him? But no! The two stallions had backed

50

to the trees, one on each side of the grassy flat, and were regaining breath and strength. They were each bloodstained in places, but neither of them were much hurt. Perhaps they might go on fighting so long that Bolder, the killer, might find himself exhausted before he could kill. However, when the fight started again. Bolder was making a much more determined attack – and much nastier. He had apparently got tired of trying to wear Baringa down.

Baringa did not seem worried.

They fought on and on. Twice Bolder got a strong grip with his teeth: twice Baringa flung him off. Several times Baringa got a grip of Bolder, and each time *he* was thrown off. They were too evenly matched, but it had become quite clear that if Baringa made a single mistake, Bolder would kill him.

By the time the sun had passed its zenith, it was also becoming clear that it might be necessary for Baringa to kill Bolder.

Yarolala was becoming desperate. Here, on this little tree-encircled flat, there was no place for Baringa to force Bolder off a cliff, as she knew Thowra had done to a horse called Arrow, years ago. Here, on the snowgrass, he was going to have to kill him with his own hooves, his own teeth, and if he did not do it, now, she was sure he would be killed by Bolder himself, and the crows would eat the flesh from his bones.

The stallions fought and fought. The sun dropped lower into a band of cloud. Several times they drew back and watched each other, their breath seeming to batter throats and chests, their blood running more freely now from bites and kicks. Sometimes they drank from the small creek. Yarolala could tell that Baringa had become angry. After all, he had done nothing to earn the savageness of Bolder's attack.

At last both horses were nearing exhaustion. Once Baringa slipped, and Bolder's fierce onslaught made it even clearer that he would kill if he was not killed or severely damaged himself.

The snowgrass was torn up and the loose soil flew in dust all around. The horses were fighting desperately, each trying to finish off the fight before complete exhaustion claimed him. In the fading light, the rose-red of the sky coloured the dusty air. Blood coloured the horses. Suddenly Bolder made a gigantic spring. He had Baringa: he was pressing him to the ground.

Panic seized Yarolala. It seemed certain that Baringa would be killed. Just as she had found him, a horse who had no reason to fight him was going to kill him ... but Baringa rose with all his strength and shook Bolder off.

For quite a while Baringa made no attack, but rested, just keeping himself from being damaged. Bolder must have thought he was becoming really exhausted because he redoubled his efforts to kill. Yarolala could see that Baringa had recovered a little.

At last Bolder made a rather wild rush at him. Baringa moved very slightly to one side and then swung round and fastened on to Bolder's wither. This time he had him too firmly to be shaken off, but the two horses still struggled on in the rosy dust. Evening came and they were still locked together, though not moving as much. It was impossible for the terrified Yarolala to see which horse had a grip of the other. It was dark when she saw the two shadow horses sink to the ground and then fall apart, their limbs setting in strange attitudes.

Hidden amongst the trees, Yarolala gave an anguished call. She stood there, shaking, for some minutes, but the two shapes of horses never moved, and already seemed to be taking on the rigidity of death.

Suddenly, possessed by horror, Yarolala turned and started to gallop away from the smell of dust and blood, and from the two bodies.

Seven

Yarolala needed all the courage of the Yarraman breed – all the brains too. Horror and fear must be kept under control. She stopped her mad gallop through the night – stopped dead – then almost stopped breathing. Someone was galloping along the track towards her. She must get off the track to Quambat and hide.

Her heart was pounding, and she trembled all over, but she stepped carefully to one side of the track, turned in towards the river, and then in the direction of Quambat again, walking as quietly as possible.

The thundering, galloping horse was coming closer. Yarolala, frightened almost more than she could bear, kept walking, parallel with the Quambat track along which he galloped, but keeping herself well hidden in the trees.

The horse went pounding past.

Yarolala stood still for a moment, shaking violently, then she turned through denser bush towards the Limestone Creek. She would cross it, keeping away from all tracks, find somewhere to hide for the night, and make her way back to Quambat later. Though there had been no other horse with her when she left Quambat Flat, then she had been seeking Baringa. Now she was completely alone. No hope, no scent upheld her. In the end, when she knew this stallion was not returning, she would have to go back to Lightning.

The thud of galloping hooves stopped, and instead of it she heard the sound of rushing water. The night was even emptier than before. Every leaf that touched her hide sent terror through her. She came to the stream. Somehow it seemed that if she could cross that, the horse might never find her. She would walk a little downstream in the water so that if he followed her scent right to the edge, and then crossed, there would be no scent on the bank just opposite.

The water was ice-cold, the current strong. Even near the edge, the force of the stream tore at her fine legs, and it was difficult not to fall among the boulders.

A flying phallanger barked somewhere above her. Yarolala jumped and snorted. Fear walked all around her and within her. There was fear in the moving water, as it caught the rather dim starlight and glittered black, fear in the silence, fear in the sound, fear, oh fear in the sudden sigh of a rising wind.

She decided to cross the creek, and immediately found herself floundering in far deeper water than she had expected. It had been a hot day: the sky was indeed partly hazed by cloud, and now the wind moaned far away in the hills above. Perhaps the weather was changing again, snow melting higher up.

Yarolala forced her way through the bitter stream. She would follow the creek down for a while, till she found a good place, and then hide herself and wait to find out, if she could, what the horse was doing.

There was also fear in the thought that she might lead another stallion to Quambat. Perhaps it was the black, owner of the five roans that Lightning had stolen.

Presently she heard him coming slowly back – so slowly that he must be nose to ground, trying to pick up her scent, but the sound of the water made it difficult to tell exactly where he was. Then she knew he was quite close to the creek, but upstream, where she had first entered it.

She began to tremble so violently that she thought she would give herself away if he came near. The teatree around her moved: she must indeed give off the scent of fear ... but how could she stop being afraid?

She heard the horse crossing the stream, and heard his hooves clattering on the stones as he shook the water from his coat. Now she must be still, still ... Yarolala called up all her courage – the courage with which generations of her ancestors had galloped over the sunlit mountains by day, the starlit mountains at night, forced their way through the snows of winter, fought, lived and loved.

She quieted her trembling and waited.

The horse moved off further from the creek, and she could only just make out his shape, for he was indeed as black as night. Perhaps he thought she had kept going straight away across country.

The tenseness went out of Yarolala's muscles. She felt very tired and without hope. She sank down on to the soft ground among the teatree.

In front of her eyes the fight seemed still to be continuing ... Baringa rearing, striking, Baringa, silver and beautiful, dancing round and round that rangy chestnut ... Half-sleeping, wholly exhausted, she dreamed of the silver horse, image after image seeming to float in the air before her, and then sometimes she was still following his scent. Once the ghost of a silver horse, blood-stained as he had been, seemed to flit through the teatree, and there was the illusive scent.

She became completely awake as she heard the black returning, smashing around through the bush. He passed fairly close; he went; he came back. All night through he roamed among the trees and scrub around the creek.

Yarolala must have gone to sleep before dawn, for she was woken by the heavy wing beat of a magpie and then its lovely carolling. There was no other sound except the birds. An occasional rustle would only be a possum retiring to sleep, or a wombat going slowly through the undergrowth to his burrow. Once she heard the thump, thump of a kangaroo hopping. She could not hear anything to indicate whether the black stallion were close or not.

She was afraid to move, and yet she wanted to go far away from the bodies of the two horses.

"Wait," something seemed to say to her, and then she told herself: "Go. There is nothing near."

She listened and listened. No sound came, other than the bush noises and the rush of the water.

She began to move forward, easing cramped limbs, pressing through the teatree. Then she heard the sound of hooves – not four hooves, but eight! She sank back into her thick covering, but this time in a place from which she could see the stream. There she stood, watching. At last out of the long-leafed black sallee trees there stepped the black stallion followed by a little, round, white mare.

Yarolala stared. Even in the short time that she had been at Quambat Flat she had heard murmurs of Baringa's beautiful mare, Dawn, and also she had heard the emus say: "He has mares who are the sun and the moon to him.

Had Baringa lost his mares to the black stallion and come searching for them, only to be killed by Bolder?

Just then the black blew through his nose, a queer, half-fearful snort, almost as though he smelt the horrifying smell of blood, and away he went, followed, more leisurely, by the round, white mare.

He seemed to go off in such a purposeful way that Yarolala decided she would try once more to go to Quambat Flat. She wriggled out of the teatree and went straight into the water without ever wondering what scent the black had found and followed.

The stream was even higher, and she noticed clouds overhead. She crossed with difficulty and rejoined the Quambat track. It was because she saw the black's churned-up hoof marks on the track that she went on the grass at the side. It would be better if she left no track.

She hurried along, and as she hurried she began to feel afraid. Perhaps the black stallion might come back; something dreadful must be going to happen; everything seemed wrong; Baringa was dead. Then the rain started to fall.

The day had been warm and now the rain was very cold. It came faster and faster. Yarolala's forelock and mane were matted and dripping. Her chestnut coat was streaked with water and dirt. For a while she sheltered in a thick grove of wattles, but even if it poured with rain, she knew she would rather keep moving and get to Quambat – the only place where she belonged at all.

She was soaked, tired and miserable when she reached the lower end of Quambat Flat. There was no movement on the clear country. Lightning and his mares were among thick trees. She caught sight of Goonda's very pale roan foal first and then saw Lightning himself, further back in the trees. Cloud and Mist, and Cirrus were nowhere to be seen.

Yarolala did not know how Lightning might behave towards her. She stood miserably in the rain, gazing up the flat towards him, and only felt the loss of Baringa more strongly.

At last she walked sadly and slowly up the flat because there was nothing else for her to do, and, as she walked, the great drops solidified into wet snow-flakes.

Lightning and his mares were all shivering, with eyes half shut against the flakes, so that no one saw her.

In a very few minutes her chestnut back was covered with wet snow, and snow was thick in her forelock, on her eyelashes. She plodded on.

It was Goonda who saw her first, saw the dejection in her walk.

Had the emus been right – that Baringa wanted no other mares? No other mares except . . . ? She wondered what other mare except Dawn Baringa did have. When Yarolala was temporarily hidden behind a few trees, Goonda moved off, as though wandering aimlessly, and joined her.

Lightning noticed Goonda go drifting down the flat, because Goonda had become so beautiful that he looked at her often, but he did not follow. There was no reason why he should leave the shelter of the trees. No danger would come to Goonda today, in all the rain and snow.

Thus it was that Goonda found Yarolala first – saw her before she expected to be seen, with her head drooping almost to the ground, and the snow, which she had not bothered to shake off, lying thick on her back.

She jumped so violently when she heard Goonda that it was quite clear that she had been very afraid as well as miserable. Goonda walked up and extended her gentle red nose to touch Yarolala's. Then she rubbed her roan neck over the top of the snow-covered chestnut neck with its silver mane, and presently began scratching and nibbling at the snow which clung to the chestnut hair.

Yarolala moved closer to Goonda for company, and soon began rubbing her head against her. Neither of them noticed Lightning coming through the snow, the big, feather flakes dense around him, but suddenly he was there, a great, silver stallion, and Goonda knew by Yarolala's trembling and the despair in her eyes that something terrible must have happened.

Lightning had been feeling very angry with Yarolala, perhaps insulted by her obvious preference for Baringa, but what was the use in being angry? If he nipped at her and was cross, she might just vanish again. Also his beautiful Goonda stood right beside her . . .

"Come back to the herd," he said, and the two mares followed. Only Goonda suspected that Yarolala had nowhere else to go.

The other mares could not help noticing how miserable she looked. It was not just the snow matting her mane and forelock and her silver tail that flew so free when she galloped. They knew that Yarolala was deeply unhappy.

Even when the sun came flashing on the snow the next morning, melted it away, made everything seem to become green and growing, Yarolala did not bother to eat, and her coat only looked rougher.

Goonda felt very sorry for her and stayed close all day.

Lightning stayed close too, because he rarely went far from Goonda, and because he felt sure that Yarolala knew some

57

very strange things, and he was extremely curious.

The roan mares were curious too, because they felt fairly sure she had been down to the Limestone.

The next day was sunny again. Cloud and Mist with Cirrus and her silver foal, were back at the top of the flat, basking in the hot sun. Several patches of sarsaparilla were suddenly covered with purple flowers. The grass was sweeter. Lightning felt as though he owned this marvellous, brightening world.

Yarolala neither ate nor moved around much.

She did not seem to notice that the others were all watching her. Slowly, but very definitely, the feeling had grown among the other mares that Yarolala had some frightening secret. They all knew she had gone to find Baringa, and that she had come back dejected and alone. As they saw her coat grow rough and her eyes become duller each day, they began to say to each other:

"What has happened? Perhaps Baringa is dead?" And they waited and wondered, and waited.

Almost the only action Yarolala had taken was to snap at Lightning if he came too close, but after a day or two she even ceased to do that. Lightning thought it might be safe to ask her what had happened down south. Even he had heard the mares whispering. So he asked Yarolala.

The only answer he got was:

"I saw the black stallion who owned the roans. He has a white and silver mare, too."

Lightning was amazed – a white and silver mare! Had the black beaten Baringa? Then he felt cold fear.

It was Goonda to whom Yarolala at last told the story of the terrible fight she had seen, and when Lightning saw Goonda's sorrow he felt quite sure that Baringa was dead. At last he could bear it no longer.

"Is it Dawn with the black stallion?" he asked Yarolala. "Is Baringa dead?"

"Bolder and Baringa are both dead," she answered.

Lightning was standing there in the bright sunshine, his coat gleaming with life. Now his ears trembled, he snorted, and every muscle stiffened. Bolder dead! Baringa dead!

Yarolala moved off, pretending to graze. At last Lightning shivered and followed her, presently rubbing his nose against her shoulder with a gentleness which she had not expected.

Lightning felt a horrid sensation of fear and uncertainty. How could Baringa, so full of life – Baringa who had often appeared when he most needed help – be dead? *How* were Baringa and Bolder both dead? Who had killed them? It must be the black, and he must have Dawn ... Lightning wanted Dawn more than anything.

All the rest of that warm spring day, he stayed beside Yarolala. Goonda stayed close too. Lightning was kind and gentle, and by nightfall Yarolala was actually eating a little grass.

A cool south wind sprang up with the night: they sheltered among trees, but even then its touch through the coat, through the mane, was disturbing.

Whispering came the wind, cold, ruffling silver hair. And the word of the wind told of far-off places, unknown hills, unknown valleys, and of drumming hooves, and speed. For Lightning the wind seemed also to carry an impression – never really taking form – of the loveliness of Dawn, and of the fury of the black stallion, an impression of death by fighting, and fear, and horror, but always the impression of Dawn, Dawn ... At last the certainty that he must have Dawn overpowered fear and horror. The cool wind touched him again and whispered of thrilling galloping on unknown mountains.

Lightning went in the night.

The cool wind blew all night long, so that a horse felt strong, trotting through it, strong enough to go on over the mountains for ever. Lightning went towards the Limestone at a very fast trot, travelling through shadow and black dark, through the fragrance of the bush at night, hearing the call of mopokes, the qua ... a ... ark of possums.

The sensation of fear and horror was still sufficiently close to make him more cautious as he got nearer to the Limestone Creek. Right at its junction with the river he paused, because he was nearing the country where he might find the black stallion, and because there just could have been a sound. ... He stood among some wattles and listened. Even to Lightning the silence seemed strange – the mopokes and possums were quiet – but Baringa would have felt with every sense that something else was listening too.

The other stallion was black, and invisible in the night. Lightning began to feel a shivering go down his spine. He waited and waited in the wattle clump. The absence of all bush sounds made the night itself seem filled with waiting danger.

If that black stallion had killed Baringa and Bolder, the killer . . . but he must have Dawn.

Then he heard a faint sound – and he felt fairly sure it came from the other side of the river. The sound was moving upstream on the far bank. . . . Hooves squelching on wet ground? Horses brushing through thick scrub? Lightning began to walk warily up his side of the creek.

He began to get more and more tense. Sometimes he could hear whatever it was, and sometimes he could not. Perhaps, if it were a horse, the hooves were soundless on soft ground. . . . Then Lightning grew tenser still. Could it be that the other was stopping and listening too – listening to him? He waited. There was silence: then the other – or was it two? – walked on. Silence again. Then as the faint sound of movement started up, Lightning stepped carefully forward.

Gently placing each hoof down, he went on: stopping and listening: walking a few steps: stopping, wondering, always kept going by the burning wish for Dawn. Otherwise it might really have been wiser to put off any possible meeting with the black stallion, whose mares he had stolen, at least until daylight, when the black would be plainly visible.

There came the sound of hooves splashing in water, clattering on stones. Definitely more than the hooves of one horse were splashing through shallow water. Then there was only the sound of the stream. The water was deep, in the middle, Lightning knew. He hurried to the bank, wondering what was happening, slipped at the edge, and made a loud clatter on the rocks, but did not slide right out into the open.

He peered through the teatree at the fast-moving water, oily in the darkness. It was just possible to see the dark shadow of a horse in midstream, and to realise that the dark horse had heard the noise of his slip, because he was standing quite still, staring in Lightning's direction. The more easily seen white mare kept on forcing her way through the deep water, not caring what noise she made. Most of her body was submerged, but Lightning just had time to realise that she did not look like Dawn, before the black started to move again – move straight towards him – and as he came, never took his eyes off the place where Lightning stood.

He must see through the teatree, Lightning thought – unaware that, for a second, one silver leg had just faintly showed – and he pressed himself quietly backwards, then moved away, quite fast, while the black was still forging on through the flooded stream.

All thought of Dawn was temporarily gone. Lightning was sure the white mare was a stranger, and he only thought of escaping as quickly as he could.

When he heard the sound of the black getting out of the water, he slowed down and crept through the teatree and wattle scrub. The black thudded and crashed around for a while, and then seemed to be heading towards the track. Lightning had absolutely no wish to get into a fight with him, and stayed quite quiet.

Grey dawn began, and when the light had become strong enough, Lightning saw him and saw his white mare, a bluish shadow beside him – a round, plump shadow.

It was certainly not Dawn, and, just as certainly, the black looked a fierce and arrogant fellow. Lightning had fought lots of fights in the last two years, and won most. He had plenty of confidence that he was the most magnificent stallion in the mountains, and was sure, or nearly sure, that he could beat anyone, but there was no point in seeking a fight with this very strong-looking horse – much better to slip away and find Dawn, for Dawn must become his.

The horse, having found nothing, gave a disgusted, angry sort of snort, and suddenly – to Lightning's amazement – started furiously down the river again, but this time on the eastern bank.

Lightning hastened back to Quambat, and only when he had gone a few miles did the creeping feeling leave the hide of his back.

All the usual Quambat horses were grazing on the flat, as he got there, except for one. A big dun stallion was missing. Lightning had beaten him in a fight, about eighteen months

61

ago, and never taken any notice of him since. Had he heard the whisper that Baringa was dead? Had he remembered playing with Dawn when she was a dancing slip of silver light, and gone to find her now?

Lightning hastened up the flat to Goonda and Yarolala.

"Where has the dun gone?" he asked Goonda, barely waiting to touch her nose.

Goonda looked troubled.

"I don't know, but every mare, every horse is saying that Baringa is dead. Perhaps he went to look for Dawn."

"Which way did he go?"

"He went in the night."

Lightning trotted off to the dun's usual camping place under a candlebark. Baringa, he knew, would have been able to track him from there, but though he searched for his hoof marks for a long time, he could not find them, so he did not know which way to go.

Lightning, in fact, had no idea where Baringa ran except that he knew he used to go up on to the Pilot and had definitely come down off that mountain, the day they went seeking Yarolala together.

There really were only two possible places, he thought, the Pilot and Dale's Creek.

Dale's Creek was where he had seen Yarolala with the emus: Dale's Creek was burnt into his memory by the fire; Dale's Creek was an eerie, quiet place that made one's coat prickle, a place where few birds sang.

Lightning set off for the Pilot.

Eight

The usual way to the Pilot lay up through Cloud's grazing ground. Lightning was wondering, as he went up, if Cloud – sire of Dawn and head of Quambat for years – knew where Baringa ran, wondering if he dared ask him? He knew that Cloud had been angry each time he had tried to take Dawn

from Baringa. Cloud had never seemed to realise that he was
the finest stallion and that Dawn should have wanted to run
with him.

A lot of the day had passed when Lightning got up to the
top of the flat. Cloud, with his mare, Mist, and his sister,
Cirrus, were standing in the sunlight, but the old horse did not
look as serene as usual.

Lightning was too anxious to find Dawn – and possibly
that other one, if Baringa really had captured her – to worry
about what Cloud was thinking, so he trotted up to them, and
only just remembered his manners.

"Hail, O Cloud," he said, and then waited, because how
could he be sure that Cloud knew Baringa was dead?

Cloud also waited.

The two stallions looked at each other and the two mares
looked at them. Even Cirrus's foal watched curiously.

At last Lightning started to move on. Cloud said nothing
at all, for he did not know what would be the best for his
daughter, Dawn and his other daughter, if it were true that she
really existed and had been won by Baringa. He felt, too,
that Lightning had stored up trouble for himself and all at
Quambat by stealing those roan mares. Cloud knew well that
the black stallion was an ill-tempered horse. He could not
think of any reason why the black had not already arrived
at Quambat Flat, looking for his mares. The only thing of

which he felt certain was that Dawn would pick her own stallion, if Baringa were really dead. Cloud mourned Baringa, because he loved the younger horse.

Lightning, made rather less confident by Cloud's disapproving silence, jogged steadily through the bush until the country became too steep and too thickly suckered, when he slowed up.

Shadows of strange horses flitted through the thick snow-gums and through the oblique bars of sunlight, the bands of shade. Lightning wished he knew some of them instead of feeling like an unwanted stranger in this country where he had rarely been before. He had no very pleasant memories of this area, either, for it was here, when he was only a two-year-old, that the grey stallion, Steel, had chased him ... here, in fact, where Baringa had saved him by calling aloud to distract Steel. That Lightning had beaten Steel afterwards, and taken the best of his mares, had not wiped away the memory of that terrifying sunset gallop.

Lightning was not exactly thinking of it now, as he pushed through the thick suckers and went out on to the open ridge, but the picture of the country had been stamped on to his mind with fear, so that though he was now a mature stallion and not a frightened two-year-old as he stepped out into the open, among the rocks and low bushes, and the purple patches of sarsaparilla all glowing with life in the late sunlight, a slow feeling of apprehension began to seep right through him.

It was nearly sunset now. Soon he would become a burnished golden horse, just as he had on that evening – a golden horse standing out for all to see on the empty hillside. The only thing that was different was the odd patch of snow lying in little gullies.

The rocks rolled under his feet and went thudding, booming, crashing through the quiet and empty air. That noise, too, would draw attention to him – but why should he feel fearful? Why, when no horse could beat him, should fear come on the cool air?

He constantly looked behind, but nothing followed him. He looked below, but there was nothing there. Only a sparrow hawk hovered out in the air above Dale's Creek, and far away, almost over the Murray, he could see two wedgetail eagles, like specks in the sky. That was all. Above, on the mountain, there was no living thing to be seen. He was entirely alone.

Hoof on rolling rock, hoof on grey, granitic soil, knee brushing bitter pea bush, muscles in the back straining – Lightning went on, with ever the cold touch of fear, until, pushing upward with his strong quarters, he was over the last climb, and stepping into a grassy glade on top.

Then all around him the Pilot's dead and silver forest wove wind-streaming limbs – countless silver trees, all dead and stiff in the form into which the wind had blown them when they lived, long years ago – and Lightning was a silver horse moving through them, afraid of he knew not what.

The sun had already set and the light itself was chill silver. He walked very slowly, each footfall silent on the grass, and he looked to either side, looked ahead, and constantly looked back. Cold and biting, the evening south wind sprang up from Suggan Buggan way. He shivered, and his shiver was not entirely from the cold. It was no wonder Baringa had chosen this place, he thought, and if Dawn were still here, she would be part of the petrified forest, and difficult to see – Dawn or that other one.

He wandered through the bleached trees, jumping nervously whenever the wind moved the branches so that they rattled together. He felt sure that someone or something was hidden in the trees, yet there was no trace of horses having been there. Where, he wondered, had the dun stallion gone, he was not here.

He went out of the dead trees and was among the living, the small, wind-tortured trees that grew almost up to the bare summit. On he walked, slowly, hesitatingly, along the grassy glades. He knew that Dawn had once been here, but he was less certain that she was here now. Whatever he had felt so strongly present in among the trees was surely only loneliness. He reached the summit and went right to the top of the rocks. Baringa had stood there, he knew, but Baringa was dead. The wind, unbroken by any tree or higher peak, was the cold, touch of this loneliness.

There were huge thunderheads just starting to boil up to the north-west, the weather changing swiftly as it does in the spring. If the south wind died down, a storm might come.

Lightning turned, stumbling on the rough rocks, and hurried down. He went to the south-eastern edge of the long summit ridge and stared down into the tangle of bush. It looked empty also, but he well knew that it probably hid many horses. Perhaps Dawn was there. He searched along the ridge till he found a track down. Soon he was enclosed in the dense bush, unable to see out, and dropping downwards fast. It would be a long climb up. Perhaps there was some lovely river flat down below, hidden by this thick bush, where Baringa had hidden, and where his mares were still grazing, waiting and waiting for him to come home.

On this side of the mountain there were many more drifts of snow still remaining, and the track was wet and slippery. Sometimes Lightning almost slid on his haunches. He was getting rather worried. He had never been so far on his own, and it would soon be dark.

He came to a small grass clearing where there was a spring and the start of a creek. He dropped his nose to drink at the first small pool – silver nose touching dark water – and suddenly saw two distinct sets of hoof prints. With his nose still in the water, but not drinking, he stared at the hoof marks. Eight marks! Small, neat! Surely they were made by two young mares!

Lightning quickly sucked up some water and then, nose to ground, started to follow the spoor. Since there was only the one narrow track in the thick bush, this was not difficult, at least not while there was light, but darkness was coming. He hastened on, only looking now and then to make sure the two sets of hoof marks were still going down the track. The track on the wet, black earth was in darkness before the day had completely gone. He knew that the spoor he had been following were not really fresh, perhaps nearly two days old, and there was no scent.

Night seemed to rise up from the ground and it closed in. He knew he would have to stop in case there were tracks branching off, and he missed the way the spoor went. As soon as he stopped he felt the immensity of the bush all around, and he wished he had Goonda with him.

There was no sound in the darkness. He got off the track and pressed himself into the bush, to stand and wait for daybreak, to stand and perhaps sleep.

At the start of the night, the stars shone brightly in the strip of sky which he could see, but as the hours spun by, clouds began to pass over.

Lightning felt as though everything around him grew larger and larger. At last he could no longer bear the silence and aloneness, and he raised his head and called. He heard his own neigh ringing out to the sky, echoing off unseen hillsides, and then the silence that followed it, because there was no answer at all.

If those young mares were anywhere near, surely they would answer. He tried again, this time throwing out to the wide air a call that held all the excitement and enticement that he, Lightning, son of Thowra, the most beautiful horse in the mountains, could offer.

Once again the echoes came back, from further and further, and as the last one died away, deep silence settled down.

The night grew darker with cloud – darker, deeper – and Lightning's confidence in himself as the most beautiful horse, and the unbeatable stallion of Quambat Flat, became less and less. He barely slept at all. Once a mopoke called and he jumped so hard that a broken branch stuck into his rump. Then, when he was almost asleep, vague, uneasy pictures of that ill-tempered black stallion kept floating through the night, so that real sleep never came. He wished he were already headed back for Quambat.

At last the light started to filter through the trees – and there were those hoof marks leading him on towards the head of the Berrima River, the hoof prints of lovely, dancing mares, that in his mind kept taking the shape of Dawn and that other one – white and silver mares dancing – so that the prints had infinite attraction. Lightning kept following for hours, without thought.

The little creek ran into another small stream which was the head of the Berrima. Here other tracks led in several directions. The hoof marks which Lightning had been so carefully following seemed to vanish. He searched desperately because he felt quite certain they were Dawn's and that other filly's. Finally he found that they had crossed the stream and gone up, not down, on a very faint track on the other side, up on to the Berrima Range.

While he had been searching for the spoor he had time to realise how heavy the clouds were becoming. He had again begun to feel that he was a long way from home: then he found the tracks again and forgot everything except the certainty that he must soon find Dawn. His moments of anxiety, however, made him go faster now, faster and faster, panting upwards on a track that grew very faint – but still held the hoof marks. The faster he went, the further he got from home.

At the top of the Berrima Range, once again there were several tracks. A wide, well-defined one went along the top, and on it were many hoof prints. The tracks which Lightning was following went straight over the ridge and down the other side.

Once again, as he paused, Lightning noticed how the clouds were massing. Then down he plunged through the thick timber, and went trotting down the track, slipping and sliding when it got wet.

He heard black cockatoos screaming with unearthly cries overhead, but he did not have time to think that a storm was surely coming.

He trotted into a clear valley with a small creek in it, and this, in turn, ran into a larger valley and a larger stream. All tracks vanished in the thick snowgrass. Lightning stood, head thrown up, looking around. There was no sign of any mares – no horses at all.

A hot wind came in gusts. In the distance he heard the rumble of thunder. The wind lifted the silver mane on the strong crest of his neck. Suddenly the sensation of being completely alone filled him, just like it had filled him during the night. Then, the hoof marks were only hidden by darkness, now they were far more hopelessly lost in the thick snowgrass. Though he had followed them for miles, he had not found the mares who had made them, and he was far from home. He neighed a long, lonely neigh.

There was no one to see the big silver stallion, no one to hear his call. He walked to the edge of the river, found a crossing place, and splashed through. There were many hoof marks in the mud and at the edge of the river, which had been much higher recently. Lightning studied them all, but could not find the two lovely sets of prints. He went back to

68

search through the grass for another path, but the grass grew too thickly.

The wind came again, and the thunder sounded closer, rolling among rocks, echoing off the heavy clouds. Lightning stood alone in the empty valley of the Ingegoodbee, and called and called.

The only living things that seemed to take any notice of him came stepping and swaying out of the bush.

Lightning started with fright, but he realised immediately that they were the emus, the same emus.

The birds came quite close, and they looked him up and down.

"What on earth are you doing here?" they asked.

Lightning looked angry for a moment, and then thought that politeness might get him further.

"I have been following Dawn's spoor," he said.

"*Dawn's!*" The emus looked completely surprised, and Lightning knew that their amazement was real. All of a sudden he realised that he had been quite wrong. After all Dale's Creek must be the place where Baringa ran.

"Is Dawn in Dale's Creek?" he asked.

The emus were still looking amazed.

"You do believe that nothing can ever befall you, don't you?" one emu said. "Why are you so far from the mares you stole? That black will assuredly come for them, and if you are not there, what will stop him taking all your mares."

Lightning simply snorted his disdain. However, he felt very uncomfortable. The quickest way home was the way he had come, over the Pilot, so he turned that way as soon as the fierce-looking birds had gone.

After a moment or so he began to canter, and, even when the track began to go up through the bush, he kept trotting as best he could. Instead of a picture in his mind of dancing white mares, he could only think of that black stallion at Quambat Flat. He did not want those roan mares to go back to their black, but, most of all, he could not bear to think of losing his beautiful Goonda.

Thunder was rumbling closer than ever, as he scrambled up the last steep part of the track on to the Pilot and into the silver forest. The wind streamed through the trees. Lightning stood still, thinking that something moved, but it was only the wind and the cry of the wind through the trees. The afternoon was getting dark, hours before nightfall. Lightning began to hurry through the forest, cantering along a grassy glade till thick, dead, silver trees stopped him.

For a moment he seemed to be yarded by the interwoven limbs and trunks which were all glittering in an oblique light that shone from a narrow space between the clouds. Lightning backed out as the strange light died away, and thunder crashed again.

The more he hurried through the forest, the more he seemed to get entangled with the stiff, dead limbs which were vibrating in the wind. He entered another grassy glade and he galloped. At last he was through those ghostly trees, and bounding down the slopes of the Pilot.

Lightning was not a naturally sure-footed horse, but now he was more than half-afraid – afraid of the storm, of the loneliness, of the death that had claimed Baringa, of the lurking menace in the black stallion – so he went leaping down the steep slopes, sending rocks and stones flying, but the thunder was louder than all the noise he made.

Sometimes he was going far faster than he meant to go, quite unable to check his speed on the rolling stones and the loose earth: sometimes he bounded in proppy, stiff-legged jumps from one rock slab to another. And the last shafts of light that often came between the clouds as the sun set, shone in his eyes, made his coat glitter. The gusty wind fanned mane and forelock, dried sweat, as the huge silver horse went madly jumping, sliding, crashing down the hillside.

His heart was pounding, sweat dripped off his neck and belly, and he was gasping for breath when he at last reached the bottom. Once he was back in familiar country, his fears quieted down.

He trotted through the bush towards the track that went between the Tin Mine and Quambat Flat, and was just starting along it, homewards, when he saw two young colts walking in his direction. He knew these two quite well. They were not much more than yearlings, two half-brothers who usually played at the lower end of the flat.

They would know whether all was well at Quambat. If

the black stallion had not gone to Quambat before the storm started, it was unlikely that he would come seeking his mares in all this thunder, and, now that he had come so far, Lightning felt that he might as well go to Dale's Creek, provided all was well with his herd.

He stopped the colts.

"Greetings," he said. "Is everything peaceful at Quambat Flat, or has a black stallion from Limestone been there?"

"Greetings, O Lightning," they replied. "Nothing has disturbed us. No black stallion has come. Everyone is restless, that is all, restless because they have heard that Baringa is dead."

Lightning thanked them and watched them go on their way, then, feeling quite certain of Goonda's safety, he turned into the bush towards Dale's Creek.

As he dropped lower, the thunder seemed to reverberate among the mountains all around. He had the feeling that he must hurry, though he knew that his mares were still quite safe, and, anyway, as soon as he was down on to the creek, in that secretive place of teatree and black sallee trees, the same haunting fear began to creep into him, the haunting fear that always came to him when he was in this valley. Now the silence was continually broken by the rolling thunder. Lightning hurried.

So far there was absolutely no sign of any other horses. Daylight would go soon and he must hurry, hurry, hurry.

There was a small patch of bare earth and for a little way he could see a track going down the valley. He went forward quickly, to look for hoof marks, and there was a set of broad, strong prints, there on the bare patch, and leading on down the track.

Lightning should have known the dun's spoor, but he did not. However, he felt convinced that these prints were his, and he followed them at a canter.

The path faded out, but every now and then it was there for a few yards, faded again, and then reappeared, all the way down the creek, and each time he found it, the hoof marks were on it.

Though he was hurrying so much, Lightning did notice that there were no other tracks about, no fresh droppings.

The evening was closing in with great claps of thunder. Soon darkness would come completely, and as it grew more difficult to see the hoof marks, Lightning began to feel more and more uncomfortable. Without realising that he was doing so, he started to go slower, and he looked around a good deal more, peered into the teatree clumps before going through them, stopped and listened.

The thunder made it almost impossible to hear anything else, but if the rumbling and crashing stopped, the silence was intense and fearful.

At last Lightning could no longer see the hoof prints. He had come a long way, and the wide, soft valley had closed in. On one side there was a high plateau, and on the other side the ridge went up steeply. The thunder continually rolled. The gusty wind moaned in the trees.

Was Dawn nowhere to be found in all the mountains?

Suddenly Lightning propped. There was something lying with its head in the creek.

"Baringa!" he thought, but even in the night the body was too dark to be that of a silver horse.

There was an ear-splitting crack, and the whole sky was lit up with lightning.

The dark heap became a horse, became dun-coloured . . . and never moved.

Lightning turned, and, as the valley was lit with silver light over and over again, and the thunder pealed, cracked, rolled, he galloped for home.

Nine

Long drifts of snow still lay on the hills that surrounded the Cascades Valley. They glittered in the early spring sunshine. The silver horse, trotting down between them, often gave a leap and a bound as though from sheer joy. He was a very big horse, and the wedgetail eagles, who had been high in the sky above the Murray, came floating over to see him, and dopped their wings in salute.

Thowra, the great Silver Stallion, sire of Lightning, grandsire of Baringa, had been held prisoner by the snow, in his Secret Valley, for longer than the horses down in the south. Now, just the day Lightning set forth on to the Pilot, he was out in the mountains again, light-footed and gay, intending to see how Baringa and Lightning were, intending to go to his mares, Koora and Cirrus.

He would gallop in the sun, dance and play, gallop and dance by starlight and moonshine. There was only one other horse who seemed to be part of the sunbeam or a flash of moonlight on snow – and that was Baringa.

It was Baringa whom Thowra would visit first, but he might see his beloved half-brother, Storm, on the way.

Thowra had been with Storm more recently than with Baringa. During the winter's heavy snow the two half-brothers had been caught in the Cascades and forced to make downwards on to the Murray River. There they had seen Baringa and his mares, Lightning and his herd, and even the black stallion, and then they had pushed on and on, round the mountains till they eventually got back to their own herds – a great journey even for those two great horses.

Thowra was rested now, coat gleaming, the vigour of spring and life in every movement. He leapt from one snowgrass bank of a creek to another. The rush of air, the shining water beneath him, the springiness of the snowgrass – all was exciting. He cantered down a sunny slope.

A dead snowgum down the little valley seemed to be flowering, and the huge flowers were white-backed magpies who exploded from the tree, flew up, and sang to the sun, and the sky, and the silver horse.

Thowra greeted them with a neigh, and their song rang out, accompanying his gay canter down to the floor of the Cascade Valley.

Thowra sent another neigh ringing to the birds, and then set off, up the valley, at a purposeful trot, towards the gap on the skyline, and then along the ridges and hill-tops to Stockwhip Gap where he should find Storm. It would be very good to graze for an hour or so with Storm and the main herd – half of which was really his – and perhaps to shake up and frighten the white-faced, blue stallion who now had his bimble below the gap, and whom Thowra had ever teased.

On he trotted. He saw only a very few young horses – some of them just starting to collect their own herds, all swift and vigorous and with no foals at foot to hamper a quick escape if men appeared.

A lovely dun-coloured filly, almost golden, flitted like a shaft from the sunset, through the snowgums. Thowra knew her to be a daughter of his, and he called her.

"Take heed," he neighed. "If men come, you are too beautiful."

"I am swift, O Thowra," came the answer, "and just now I am young and free."

"Free, free, free," his hoofs whispered on the soft grass – and then, as he cantered: "Young and free, young and free." And the sunlight warmed him, the breeze cooled him, a drink from a stream poured the swiftness of the blizzard into his body, for in the blizzards were the streams born.

Thowra trotted and cantered over the kingdom which he had won years ago from the grey stallion, the Brolga.

Storm had been expecting him, and when he saw the flicker of silver, the proud toss of mane, between the big, old snowgums on Stockwhip Gap, he gave a great neigh of welcome, and cantered towards him. In the herd, scattered among the trees, the little nickering whisper went round:

"The Silver Stallion," and a neat, pale blue roan filly, a daughter of Whiteface's, who had attached herself to the herd and made up her mind that she would be Thowra's, began to dance a little through the trees, towards the two huge stallions.

Thowra was far too pleased to see Storm again to take any notice. He saw that Storm looked a little older, perhaps had not completely recovered from their gruelling journey and the shortage of food. It was not just in his own imagination that Thowra was still vigorous and young. Every animal and every bird of the bush simply thought of Thowra as for ever in his prime, for ever filled with spirit.

Now the two stallions were bucking and rearing around each other with pleasure. The pale roan filly waited. Thowra looked very handsome. She was sure he must be more handsome than the silver horse about whom her father's herd were murmuring.

74

She started to romp and play with the other fillies, but as soon as Thowra stopped his game with Storm, she went out on her own again to arouse his interest, to be the one beautiful filly dancing apart on the edge of the ridge:

Thowra was too filled with his own longing to travelling the ranges, footloose, by day and by night, even to think of her twice – though of course he noticed her, because he noticed everything.

The filly, feeling annoyed that her beauty had not caught his interest, at last went down the open snowgrass valley that led to the east and towards the Charcoal Range. Her sire's herd were likely to be there, and from them she might learn more of the other silver horse, for word seemed to have come somehow, borne by the birds, or the flying phallangers, just rumours; perhaps something in the call of a kurrawong which told of the mysterious comings and goings of a silver horse, perhaps something in the sad threnody of a plover, crying of sorrow and death.

It was not because of the filly that Thowra went walking down through the trees. He could not be at Stockwhip Gap without visiting old Whiteface, teasing him a little, and finding out what were the rumours which were borne on the mountain winds, for Whiteface always seemed to hear a great deal.

He saw the filly prancing and gambolling her way down the open snowgrass, and, for the first time, he realised she was lovely, but he still did not take any real notice of her.

She knew he was walking down through the trees and she went more slowly, so that they reached Whiteface's herd at the same time. Whiteface showed very little pleasure at the sight of Thowra!

His lack of appreciation of Thowra's visit earned him a rather firm bite on one ear.

"What news flies on the wind?" Thowra asked.

Whiteface looked dumb.

"No news. We have all been too taken up with finding food."

Thowra began to cast his eye over Whiteface's herd. It was then that the filly, desperately wanting Thowra to choose her, said:

"What of the rumours of a silver stallion walking on his own? What of the whispers of death? You were all murmuring of these things only a few hours ago." She moved closer to Thowra because she had given away the news which her sire had refused him, all to get his attention.

Thowra saw another rather good-looking filly give her a spiteful nip as he said:

"Death for whom?"

"One of the young silver horses," Whiteface answered, and every line of his body said: "You'd better get going," but he was not fool enough to say it aloud.

"Which?" Thowra was suddenly more fierce and menacing than Whiteface had ever seen him.

"It is only one of those tales that seemed to be whispered by the trees," Whiteface answered, "but there may be more truth in the story that one of the silver horses was way down on the Murray alone, seeking a white mare who was once owned by the other one."

Thowra gave no further thought to Whiteface, and not another thought to the filly, but turned uphill again, towards Storm. He told Storm what he had heard, and then went straight on, headed for Baringa's Canyon.

Close behind him went the filly.

As soon as Thowra was out of sight of the herd, he began to go very fast. However fast he went, he made no sound, but the filly, having to make a great effort to keep up, made quite a noise, and Thowra heard her.

At first, when he looked back and saw her, he thought he would send her straight back, and then the idea came to him that she could look handsome in Baringa's herd. . . . Baringa could not possibly be dead, perhaps hurt, somewhere far away, and unable to get home, and what could be a better welcome home than a beautiful filly for his herd? He would take the filly with him, if she could keep up.

He waited till she was close behind him, and after that he kept looking back to see if she followed.

He did not even call in on Son of Storm, and avoided being seen by other horses, keeping off all tracks.

It was night, and very dark, when he reached the ridge above the Canyon. There he went round and round in a few circles, then down over the steepest and most rugged part, making sure the filly was close on his heels, making sure that the route he picked was really frightening so that she would be less likely to try to climb out – just as he, with his circles in the dark, had tried to ensure that she did not know where she was going.

In this pitch darkness they went into Baringa's Canyon, almost as though they were dropping down, and when they were nearly there, Thowra, who, in spite of his efforts to frighten her, was glad that the filly was following fearlessly, said.

"Either tonight, or soon, if you choose to do so, you may join the herd of the most beautiful stallion in all the mountains."

"Who, O Thowra, do you mean? To me it is you who are the most beautiful stallion."

The filly could feel the presence of Thowra in the darkness as she heard his answer.

"Not I, but my grandson, Baringa."

"Was it not for one named Baringa that the plovers cried?"

This time Thowra's answer seemed to vibrate in the invisible leaves of the ribbon gums and sallee trees:

"Baringa could not be dead."

They had not once stopped moving down the precipitous hillside. Now there were cliffs just underneath them, and the filly must have felt that something even steeper was ahead, because she pressed close to Thowra, but she never hesitated as he led down the small footholds and little platforms and cracks on the granite cliff.

They were almost at the bottom when Thowra said:

"If Baringa is not here, he will return, for he has the most beautiful herd in all the mountains, and now I am adding you to it. There is surely nothing that would be more likely to draw him back."

The filly wondered if he were really feeling less worried, or whether he was only just trying to make himself believe that all was well. Could a herd of lovely mares call a horse back from the dead? What was the faint gleam she could see in his eyes in the darkness?

She followed him closely, wondering also what sort of

reception she would get from the mares, who must be some-where quite close. A current of excitement was racing through her, too. At last she was going to run with the most wonderful horse in all the mountains – perhaps Baringa, perhaps Thowra.

All at once they landed on flat ground. She could feel through the darkness that there were others coming close. Did she imagine it, or were there the light-coloured shapes of two mares?

Thowra whinnied softly, then a gentle paw touched his nose. He dropped his great head to the grey kangaroo's.

"Benni, Benni," he said. "What has happened? Where is Baringa? Where is Dawn?"

"Dawn was swept downstream in the flood in the Murray," Benni answered, "half a moon ago, now. Baringa has gone searching for her and has not returned, though he should have been back ... unless he could not find her and he has kept on and on searching. . . . She was soon to foal. . . ."

Thowra felt suddenly cold.

"I did not hear about Dawn, but I heard that Baringa was missing," he said, "and I have brought this filly for him, when he returns. She is a half-sister of yours, Koora. She must be tired and hungry now. Could you lead her to where she may find some sweet grass? She will need a drink too," his nose touched Koora – the sweet mare who had followed him over the mountains, and would follow him anywhere, to death in fire or flood, if needs be, or to perish in the snow.

They fed and drank and, later, all stood close together for company. The little herd was glad of Thowra's presence. This was the sixth night without Baringa.

Already the weather which had been so fine, was changing, and the same gusty north-west wind that was disturbing Lightning, on the Pilot, moved in the trees above.

As they stood half-sleeping, a sound came – a sound only partly heard, not really breaking the silence of the night. Whatever it was made each animal alert and tensely waiting. Waiting. . . . Waiting. . . . Then it came, louder, closer, and this time it was the lonely neigh of a stallion, a stallion whom none of them knew.

The new filly was amazed at the sudden tension in Thowra and the others around her. This place must be far away from

78

any horses because it was obvious that they rarely heard a call, and obvious that this call meant great danger. She had felt the hair of Thowra's coat rising, as though he were listening with all himself. Then she knew he had moved away — knew that, silent as a fanning breeze, he was going towards that sound.

Thowra had heard that strange call, and all the half-formed rumours which he had heard at Stockwhip Gap, and the story of Baringa's absence from the Canyon, fitted together, and he knew that it was likely that this was a stallion who had heard Baringa was dead, and had come seeking his mares.

There was no time to lose.

Swiftly – his pounding heart filling his great, silver chest – and without making any sound, Thowra went up the bluff at the head of the Canyon.

Thowra had never been a killer, but something told him that this horse must at least be given such a beating that he would never return . . . and then, if he lived and went limping over the mountains, would every horse know that a silver stallion had risen up out of the Canyon in Dale's Creek and beaten him? Perhaps this horse should never be left to limp over the mountains. . . .

Thowra was nearing the top of the bluff. He heard that neigh ring out again and echo in the Canyon around him. It was not just a cry of loneliness, it was also a call to a beautiful mare – to Dawn perhaps:

"Where are you? Come to me."

Thowra felt fury rising within him. Baringa, who was light and life, could not be dead, and no stallion should be able to come so close to his mares. He climbed the last few feet of the bluffs, and out over the top.

There, a few feet below him, he could faintly see the lightish coat, the shape of a big horse – a very light chestnut or dun.

Thowra had hurried, but he stilled his laboured breathing, and crept slightly up the ridge and around, so that he would not seem to rise up out of the Canyon. Then he attacked the horse from behind.

The dun swung round too late, his hindfeet slipped on the muddy bank, and the two horses slid together into the creek. Water splashed up all round them, silvered by starlight.

Thowra landed on top of the other, kneeling on him. The dun was young and very strong: he was also fighting for his life. He gave a tremendous heave upwards and got to his feet, but Thowra was on a rock, towering above him, was leaping towards him.

The dun sprang away, his feet slithering on the hidden boulders below the deep, swift water. Thowra was after him through the starlit spray – a horse of sparkling water and starshine, but with the strength of the white blizzard.

The dun hurled himself at Thowra, but his feet slipped into a deeper hole. Thowra saw him try to rear up, saw him get into slightly shallower, but very swift water, and then suddenly one of his legs slipped on the rocks, and the horse fell sideways with a scream of pain.

Thowra stopped in mid-rear, dropped his forefeet on to the submerged rocks again. He saw the dun give a convulsive struggle, saw that one hind leg was wedged in the rocks, saw the strange twist in the animal's back, saw it collapse.

What Thowra could not see in the dark was the horse's head sinking under the swift, spring current.

He stood waiting, his wet coat touched by the gusty wind, making him very cold. After a few moments he stepped forward. The dun did not stir. He went closer. Only the water moved the mane.

Thowra gave a snort of fear, that fear which all horses feel at the sight of death, and he backed out of the creek, and turned for the Canyon. This horse would not even go limping over the mountains, and Thowra felt uneasy because ill luck, in the swift water, had caused his death. Might ill luck have killed others in this spring's floods?

Ten

Because the sight of death was horrible, and *this* death filled him with such foreboding, Thowra, when he started for Quambat Flat, before daylight next morning, did not go by way of Dale's Creek. He climbed Baringa's cliff on to the High Plateau.

The change in the weather was now more noticeable. Few stars showed, and the wind was gustier, stronger. As the light started, Thowra could see heavy clouds rolling up from the north-west. Being much more attuned to the weather and the country around him than Lightning was, he knew, even in the early morning, that thunder was coming. When Lightning was hurrying down to the head of the Berrima River, barely heeding the weather, Thowra trotted across the High Plateau, his hair alive to the coming storm.

Once he went right to the western edge, where a wedge of rock jutted out, and he could look down on to the Murray River. Even from that distance he could see that the river was still very swollen. He stood there for a long time, deeply anxious, watching the river, gazing at the country on the opposite bank.

In Thowra life itself was so vigorous that it was impossible for him to believe that Baringa and Dawn were dead without the proof of his own eyes seeing the bodies, or at least the proof of searching and searching and being absolutely unable to find them. The river certainly must have been overpoweringly strong when Dawn slipped in: Benni, he knew, was very fearful for Dawn's life; but Thowra felt that they both must be alive. With this feeling strongly within him, he neighed his challenge to the river and the unknown land on the other side. Then he turned, once more to Quambat Flat.

He hurried down off the High Plateau, hurried up and down the Quambat Ridge, and at last down on to the tree-fringed edge of Quambat Flat.

He could not see Lightning anywhere, and none of his mares were visible either. Thowra skirted round the flat, hidden in the trees, and going towards Cloud, Mist and Cirrus, and when he saw them he felt the pleasure that always warmed him at the sight of the gracious, old stallion, and the joy he felt in the grey mare, Cirrus, whom he had won, years ago, from Steel.

"There is trouble, trouble," Cloud said in answer to his question. "Lightning has surely gone to try to find Dawn, and sometime, without doubt, the black stallion will come to claim the mares which Lightning stole at the time of the melting of the snow." As he spoke, the thunder started its far-

81

away rumblings, and seemed to emphasise all he said. Lightning's mares were all out of sight in the thick bush on the slopes of the Cobras, Cloud told Thowra, and added that he should find Yarolala and ask her about the fight between Baringa and Bolder. He told him, too, that Lightning had headed towards the Pilot: he mentioned that the dun horse had also gone and not returned. Cloud was not serene and happy like he usually was.

Thowra went off to find Lightning's herd, still keeping himself hidden in the timber, and, as he went, the thunder sounded closer and more ominous.

At the same time as Lightning was crying his loneliness aloud to the empty hills, his sire, the Silver Stallion, walked without sound through the bush towards his herd.

Goonda was the first of the mares whom he saw, and he was amazed at how beautiful she had become. He went a little further, made out Steel's mares, then the ones that belonged to the black stallion, and finally a chestnut mare who was exactly like his own sire, Yarraman, and remembered seeing her as a two-year-old in Son of Storm's herd. She must be Yarolala.

He walked up to Goonda, going out into the open from between the red trunks of two candlebarks.

Goonda jumped with surprise, then greeted him affectionately.

"What tidings have you brought?" she asked.

"None. I have come to learn what has befallen Baringa."

"That you must find out from Yarolala. She saw Baringa die."

Yarolala had come closer, and Thowra turned to her and asked her the same question. He knew of the horse, Bolder, knew him to be a savage killer, but when she had finished her story he exclaimed:

"They *both* died!"

"Yes."

"Then that is the strangest fight of which I have ever heard," Thowra said, and stood thinking for quite a while before he asked Goonda about Lightning.

By the time Thowra had learnt all he wished to know – and told nothing to anyone, not even Goonda – the thunder was echoing off the Cobras, rolling round the Pilot, and crashing closer, closer.

Even if Lightning had gone to the Pilot to begin with, he might easily finish by going to Dale's Creek. Before starting his search for Baringa, dead or alive, Thowra knew he must make sure that Lightning did not find the Canyon. He went back round the flat, working his way round towards the Pilot Gap from where he could drop into Dale's Creek.

Goonda watched him until he vanished, and when she looked round, Yarolala had gone too.

Thowra took great care, as he dropped down into Dale's Creek. He must be sure, if he found Lightning, not to let him think that he knew where Baringa's mares were hidden. It would be best to let Lightning see that he came from Quambat – always supposing that Lightning did go to Dale's Creek.

The afternoon was closing in, heavy clouds making it very dark, and the thunder echoed off the rocks on the High Plateau. Thowra walked carefully down the valley, keeping hidden in the trees. Just before darkness came, he went through a patch of teatree on to the track. There he saw two sets of hoof marks – one, very fresh, was Lightning's.

Thowra began to go as fast as he could without giving himself away. Then came that tremendous crack of thunder and the lightning that lit the whole sky. Thowra found himself sweating with anxiety. What should he do if Lightning found his way to Baringa's Canyon?

Again and again the valley was filled with the silver-blue light of the electric storm, and thunder filled the air so that even Thowra could not hear the pounding sound of hooves.

Lightning burst out of the darkness as the valley was lit up again.

Thowra sprang from the trees and stood in his way, himself afire with the silver-blue light.

Lightning pulled up to a sliding stop, almost crashing into the glittering horse who had sired him. He was sweating with fear.

"Lightning, Lightning, of what are you afraid – not the storm, for you were born during just such a storm as this?"

"No, not the storm. The storm lit up a body. . . ."

"Lit up what body?"

83

"The body of a dead horse. A dead horse who was alive only three days ago, and he went seeking Dawn, as I was seeking Dawn. Baringa, too, is dead."

"Goonda told me to come this way to find you. She thought you might come down into this valley from the Pilot. We will go to Quambat together."

"Let us hurry away," said Lightning. "This is a valley of death."

"I know it is a valley of death," Thowra answered, "but we will not gallop, lest the whole world knows we are here. Follow me."

Lightning followed as best he could, but making much more noise than Thowra did. Thowra made no comment because he knew there were no other horses about. By the way Lightning kept on his heels or alongside, he guessed that the fear of death – and whatever had killed that horse – would keep Lightning away from Dale's Creek for quite a time.

Thowra needed time. He needed time to go and find Baringa and Dawn.

Just as they were reaching Quambat Flat, Thowra said:

"If you go wandering away from your own mares, like this, you will lose them all. The black stallion must come soon, for his own mares, and Goonda has become so lovely. . . ."

At that moment the storm lit up the whole of the flat. It seemed completely empty of horses.

Thowra, of course, knew the mares were all there, but he let Lightning get anxious. The more anxious he got about them, the less likely he was to leave them again.

By the time he saw his herd, Lightning had become so worried that he rushed up to them, filled with relief and excitement, and for a few minutes, did not realise that Yarolala had gone. By the time his excitement had burnt itself out a little, and the fear he had felt had partly come back, Thowra had gone too.

The night was so dark, except when the storm lit it up, that there was no hope of seeing where Thowra had gone.

Lightning felt most uneasy.

Soon the rain began to beat on the wind, rain that would wash out all tracks. Lightning stood beside Goonda, feeling her warmth go through him, shoulder and flank.

Thowra went deeply into the bush so that even the vivid light of the storm would not easily show him up, and he headed for the junction of the Limestone with the river. Then he intended to go up the Limestone to try to find the place where Yarolala said Baringa and Bolder had fought – and died.

By the time he reached the junction of the two streams, the rain was pouring down, obliterating all tracks. There in the bush, he waited till most of the night had gone because, for this search, he needed daylight. As soon as daybreak came, he started off.

Thowra went quite a long way up the Limestone, seeking for the body of a horse – or two bodies – hoping he would find nothing, and yet knowing that, until he saw Baringa alive, galloping, he would be unable to be sure.

He also kept a wary eye out for the black stallion.

Yarolala's description of the place where the two stallions fought had been most confused. All that Thowra knew for certain was that it was on or near the track and below huge rocks. He passed through one huge pile of slabs and tors, and went down on to the little tree-encircled flat below. The flat was quite empty.

Thowra, feeling a lightness, nosed about, but had there been any signs of a fight, the light snow that had fallen after it, and the rain that was pouring down now, would have removed them. He must go further, though, still searching, in case this was not the place Yarolala meant.

All of a sudden he saw one clear hoof mark, filling with water, and was certain that the spoor was fresh – also that it was Yarolala's. It was not going towards the track, but towards the river.

Thowra wondered whether to try to find her, if it were Yarolala, or whether to go on up the river, and decided that he must make sure there was no place further up where the bodies of Baringa and Bolder might be lying. So he followed the track again, on and on, and the further he went without finding any more heaped up rocks, the lighter he felt, and the stronger his certainty became that Baringa must be alive. He also began to wonder more when he was going to find the black stallion, never dreaming that the reason why the black had not arrived at Quambat Flat, days ago, was that the black, too, had been searching for Baringa, and was only just returning to his bimble, a little further up the Limestone.

The black had spent days on the other side of the river, had come back on that side, and had not yet crossed over. It was not he, whom Thowra saw first, but the round, white mare.

Now, Thowra's gaiety had been rising and rising with every moment in which he failed to find the body of Baringa, and the sight, through the trees that lined the banks of the river, of that round little mare, suddenly seemed to make his rising spirits explode.

Never for one moment did he think she was Dawn. He simply thought that whoever owned her, she would make another mare for Baringa. Baringa would have such a homecoming!

Then he saw the black stallion's coat, then a flickering movement through the thick trees, and saw his legs, his crested neck, his quarters – and he only thought: "What fun! Somehow I shall take the mare for Baringa!"

Thowra stayed quietly in dense teatree and watched the black lead the white mare across the stream. Then he followed them a little further upstream, watched them get in under a large candlebark as if that were a usual sheltering place. It appeared to Thowra as if they had come home. He wondered where they had been. The black was obviously in a rather bad temper, but the little fat mare did not seem to let anything worry her.

A little further down the river, Yarolala stood hidden in the same dense patch of teatree in which she had hidden after watching Baringa and Bolder fight. She had already found no sign of a dead horse on that tiny flat, and hope had suddenly sprung up within her. Now she had seen the black stallion and mare go up the river and remembered that other time when she stayed hidden in the same teatree and had heard the black go downstream. Suddenly she remembered, too, how she had lain down and, half-sleeping, had seen a vision of a blood-stained silver horse go past. How stupid she was! That blood-

86

stained horse had been no vision, but Baringa himself, going down the stream too. What had happened to him since? Had the black found him and fought him while he was weak and exhausted from fighting Bolder? Where was he now? And where should she go now?

Yarolala did not know where to go. She wanted so deeply to find Baringa and had no idea how to start. She stood wondering if she should try going down the river, if, in fact, she had the courage to do so. Also she had a sneaking feeling that Baringa did not live down the river, but somewhere closer to the Tin Mine Creek. She wished the rain would stop.

Thowra, for the moment, was thankful for the rain. It would continue to wash away tracks. He watched the black stallion and his round mare. Every time the mare moved at all, the stallion snapped at her peevishly and she took no notice at all except to stand a little further away and nibble some grass.

It was just then that some movements in the trees, a little distance away, on the splayed-out ridge, attracted the black's attention. Thowra had already seen them, and while unbothered as to who made the movements, he was almost certain that he had seen the sway of emu feathers, the outlines of neck and head.

The black was jumpy. He kept looking in the direction of those movements, and it was easy to see that very soon he would be unable any longer to stand peacefully beneath the trees, but be forced by his nervous curiosity to see what was up there.

Presently the black stallion turned to give the mare a little nip to tell her to follow, and was so wondering what was up the ridge that he did not notice that she was standing further off than usual, nor did he notice that she had got tired of following and that she simply remained under their tree.

The little white mare watched him go, thinking that he had become unbearable since his beloved roans had gone. She had just spent days and days following him, while *he* followed the idea of a silver horse whom she did not think he had ever really seen. Somehow the black had heard a rumour that a silver horse had been in his country during the heavy snow, and he had been thinking of silver horses ever since. The little mare thought the whole story was nonsense, and was sure that the black stallion had only dreamt, too, about the blood-stained silver horse for whom they had searched for days on the far side of the river.

She stood there, rather huddled in the rain, grumbling to herself, and soon did not even watch the black trotting across the hollow and up the ridge.

Why was one wet, rainy moment different from the moment before? But she felt sure she had heard the faintest call. She raised her head slightly and listened, ears flickering. There it was again, almost beyond hearing, but a call to set the blood racing. . . .

She turned round carefully. There just seemed to be a wall of trees. Then something moved, and — was she dreaming? — there was the head, the crested neck, the shoulders of a silver horse.

The horse's nose trembled again with that thrilling, half-heard call: his eyes were gazing straight at her.

The little round mare gave one quick look back at the black who was still trotting up the ridge, and then, on her toes, went towards the silver horse.

Thowra greeted her softly, and led her away through the thick bush, keeping off all tracks.

After a while the rain slackened: any hoof print made now would show. Thowra tried to persuade the little mare to place her feet carefully, but she thought it was all far too funny, and anyway, if the black came, Thowra would fight for her and beat him easily, so there was no cause for worry.

Thowra made her walk in the water for a little while, when they crossed at the junction, so that her hoof marks would not show on the mud. He thought he would take her up on to the High Plateau by way of the steep, rocky ridges from the river, and then down into Dale's Creek and around and about, so that he twisted her sense of direction — if she had one — before taking her into the Canyon.

They crossed at the junction only a short time after Yarolala had crossed and gone up on to Quambat Ridge.

Thowra and the mare had not gone far before he realised

that it might not be a very fast journey, because the round mare was undoubtedly lazy and inclined to regard everything as a joke. This irritated him rather, because he did not want to waste time. He wanted to put her safely in the Canyon and then go off and find Baringa, so he urged her along with a mixture of cajoling and teasing, beginning to wonder how stupid he was being, to bother about her ... but in fact she was rather delightful. He was glad, however, that Storm could not see them.

The black stallion had almost reached the place where he had seen the movement in the trees, instead of a young stallion – or even a silver stallion – stepping out of the snow-gums, the great bunches of feathers which were the emus, came swaying and bounding into the open.

At first the black stallion was annoyed because he had been expecting a horse, hoping for some clue to the whereabouts of his mares. Then he wondered if these birds might tell him something – not that he trusted them over much.

At first the birds looked at him in fierce and icy silence.

The black stallion did not possess very courtly manners. He asked most abruptly if they knew where his five roan mares had gone.

The emus, who loved to know everything and loved everybody to know they knew everything, drew themselves up very haughtily.

"*Your* roan mares?" they said. "We know plenty of roan mares, but yours ... ?"

"Yes mine. I have heard they were stolen as the snow melted, by a silver horse."

"Those ones! You could have stolen them back a few days ago! Where have you been?"

"I was following a silver horse down the river, but I didn't find him again, or find any mares."

"Oh," said the emus, learning something. "Which silver horse did you follow?"

"I don't know. How many are there? This horse had had a terrific fight and was all blood-stained. He went down the west bank of the river, but he simply vanished."

"A-a-h," said the emus, learning even more, and determined to tease him. "Have you lost all your mares, every one?"

The black stallion felt a wave of uneasiness go over him. He turned his head quickly. There was no sign of the white mare either behind him or under the tree. He swung round and called, but there was no answer.

With a roar of rage, he started down the hill.

The emus fluffed out their feathers, for he had no manners.

It took only a second or so for the black stallion to reach his shelter tree. He looked carefully below it and he searched the bush. There was the scent of a stallion: there were some hoof marks made by his mare, hoof marks that led into dense timber.

He tried to follow, but soon lost the tracks, and then just went on downstream, searching wildly.

It was by great good luck that the black found one mark of his little round mare's off forefoot, on the other side of the Quambat stream, just at the junction, one hoof mark pointing down the river – this time on the eastern bank.

Further on there were more, where she had loitered and teased Thowra on a muddy patch. He could smell her scent and the scent of the stallion, but never a track of the stallion did he see.

Off he went as hard as he could go, hooves slithering and squelching, picking up her track here and there, and knowing he was going faster than they were.

Eleven

It was a good thing that Thowra decided to cut up towards the Quambat Ridge a little earlier than he had first intended. He and the white mare were not far up a rocky spur, and only partly hidden in scrub, when the black stallion went pounding past, below.

Thowra watched with interest, so did the white mare.

As soon as the horse had gone well past, Thowra urged the little mare to climb faster and more quietly.

90

"Why don't you fight him?" she asked.

"It would be better not to – yet," was Thowra's puzzling reply. "And perhaps one of the others will want to."

This puzzled her still more. She tossed her head and did not move any faster at all. Thowra felt exasperated, but there was no doubt that she was rather fun, and he was so glad that Baringa was alive and he wanted to give him this pert mare.

There was a thudding of hooves again, the black was coming back.

While he rushed back along the river, trying to pick up their tracks, Thowra led his rather maddening companion through some thick trees, across a gully, and on to the next ridge. They had only just reached the ridge when they heard him below again, but he was not coming up yet, just grumbling around, trying to track them.

Thowra gave the mare a little nudge, to start her climbing, but she was watching the black through the trees, watching with far too much amusement to want to move.

Thowra nudged her again, and breathed fiercely down his nose.

All she did was nip him.

So he gave her a gentle bite, but still she would not climb. He began to understand that she thought it would be fine to have him fight for her.

The danger in the whole thing would be if, through her playfulness, they led the black too near to the Canyon.

Thowra suddenly knew what to do.

"I don't think you are worth the trouble," he said, and started to climb up the ridge on his own, but not too fast.

The mare took no notice and he went on alone. If she did not come, then, he supposed, it was better to leave her, make down on to the river again, and search for Baringa. He tried not to look back . . . she was rather sweet, there was no doubt of that.

After a while he heard her following, and she was making enough noise to fetch a stallion from miles away. Luckily the black was not right below: he had gone charging on downstream again.

Thowra slowed up a little, to give her the encouragement of getting closer, then he went on.

He reached a rocky place from which he could look out. There was still no sign of the black. This time he waited for the mare.

This time she knew he was not joking.

"If you come," he said. "You must follow more carefully. Don't leave tracks and don't make a noise," and he led her across two gullies, this time, so that if the black did find her tracks, he would be puzzled again.

The mare obeyed.

Thowra increased his pace a little, and though she was blowing, the mare kept up. They heard the crashing of a boulder. Apparently the black had started upwards and dislodged a rock. Thowra decided to cross over on to even another ridge, each time working back towards the south rather than nearer to the High Plateau.

He waited and listened for a while. The black was still coming.

Then Thowra changed his plans. He began to make down again.

When the mare asked him what he was doing, he simply said:

"Wait and see. It will give you a chance to stop puffing. You may need your breath later."

He led her right out into the open, by the river bank, and there he stood, letting out neigh after neigh. Wild, triumphant, challenging, the cry of the Silver Brumby rang out.

From high up there came a roar of anger, and presently the sound of falling rocks.

Thowra turned towards the Limestone, then, near the junction, hid himself and the mare, to watch what happened.

What happened was quite unexpected, because he had forgotten the emus.

The emus and the black stallion arrived at the junction almost at the same moment. The black was breathless, so the emus had plenty of time to make him uncomfortable with their piercing stare.

The black regained his breath, but, Thowra thought, he probably never did have any manners to regain. Manners or not, he was only intent on finding out if the emus had seen the silver horse and his white mare.

The emus looked astonished.

"*White* mare this time! Forgotten the roans already. No manners, no memory . . ."

Then . . . and Thowra was sure they took a horrible pleasure in upsetting everyone and everything . . . one emu, totally ignoring the black, said to the other:

"It's amazing that he has never thought to go to Quambat Flat."

The black seemed to stop in mid-air as he advanced, rather threateningly, towards them. He stood out-staring the fierce-eyed birds.

Thowra knew, by this, that the black had been too occupied following Baringa, to go to Quambat, but he could see that he also had not thought of going there.

Now he was not going to think much: he was going straight there. Thowra watched him heading along the track, and wondered whether to try to catch his attention before he got far, but reflected that, after all, Lightning had asked for it, and if he could not defend himself and his mares now, he should be able to. Also Lightning had had such a bad fright that it was likely he had his mares hidden somewhere.

Thowra determined to get his lazy little companion to the Canyon as fast as she could go.

He led her up Quambat Ridge, and thence to Dale's Creek, having made sure that the emus did not see them go. On the way he learnt, from hoof marks and scent, that Yarolala had gone ahead of them up the ridge. This made him wonder, but the first necessity was to get the white mare into the Canyon. Then he would have to find Baringa, then see what had happened to Lightning. He felt fairly sure that Yarolala would not find the Canyon, though it was likely that she had discovered that Baringa was not dead, and was now looking for him.

Thowra hurried on, and whenever the mare stayed too far behind, he went on alone, and she managed to go faster.

Dale's Creek, as evening drew in, was as eerie as it always was. Thowra felt its strange silence the more deeply, knowing that the dun lay dead near the entry to the Canyon. As darkness fell, he made a big circle up on to the side of the High Plateau and then another on to the flank of the Pilot, then smaller circles through teatree and splashing through the stream.

The little mare kept closer now. In the darkness she was lost and, even with her fun-loving nature, had become afraid.

At last he led her down the cliff into the Canyon.

Thowra was on his way again with the first grey light. This time he went down the cliffs into the Tin Mine Creek and then down the cliffs of that creek, and along it till he reached the river. There, at last, he found a place where he could swim across the river, and he began searching upstream, on the western bank.

Already the country had become far more springlike. He brushed through the golden and brown of the bitter pea flowers that were just coming into bloom. Many of the wattles were in full flower, and some of their golden, fluffy balls were blowing off in the light breeze, or showering down on his mane, his shoulders and back.

Suddenly he stopped short. Right under an overhanging snowgrass tussock, as though the foot had slipped, a hoof print was pressed deep into the now dry mud, and filled with the wind-blown wattle blooms that had slithered into it. Thowra dropped his head down to sniff at it. It was not a fresh print: it had been made even before the last rain, but it was Baringa's print, and it pointed downstream.

Thowra began a careful search. It was hours later, and almost dark, before he found another trace of Baringa, and that was a few silver hairs on an overhanging branch, inland from the river. Here Thowra was forced to spend the night, because darkness was useless for a search.

It was on this night that Lightning crept down from the Cobras where he had hidden his mares, and he came down because he was almost sure he had heard an unknown call echoing among the rocks. He did not go out of the fringe of trees, but stood carefully watching the flat. Even though the night was only lit by starlight, he could just make out a big, black horse moving restlessly about – or perhaps he heard him so clearly that he imagined him. Also there were some of the younger horses of Quambat, hidden in the bush, who told him that this horse had rampaged around all the day before, obviously finding track and scent of his mares, and, also obviously, here to stay till he got them.

Perhaps, by the morning light, this ill-tempered black stallion might track the herd up the Cobras. Lightning decided he would stay close to see what the horse did when daylight came.

Also coming closer in, but hidden among the trees, were the two emus, anxious to see what mischief they had caused. Deeper in the bush, Yarolala was walking quietly along.

Yarolala had gone right to the far end of the High Plateau, the day before. She had spent one lonely, frightening night pressed between two rocks, on Quambat Ridge. Then, getting more and more nervous, she had gone up on to that High Plateau where there was rarely a day in which the wind did not move, and where it seemed bad to be alone.

Every golden chestnut hair had stood on end when she found the sunken, washed-out remains of rolling holes that had not been used for months and months. Someone had not come back – and she hastened on. When she finally reached the end of the High Plateau, she had stood with the wind lifting that lovely silver mane, so like Yarraman's, and looked over the Canyon, over the deep gorge of the Tin Mine Creek, over the wild, blue ridges, right to the Main Range, and she had seen no sign of horses, only a vast depth that seemed to her a place where no horse could go.

She had gazed for a long time over the tangle of mountains and gorges, then, frightened and lonely, she had gone back towards Quambat, at least to spend the night near other horses before setting off again on her search for Baringa.

Twelve

When Baringa recovered enough to get up and leave the scene of his fight with Bolder, Bolder was still lying exhausted and considerably damaged. Baringa, himself, was trembling in every nerve and muscle. He knew he could draw up the strength to kill Bolder, even then, but he had no wish to do it. The

whole look of him was the look of a completely defeated horse. Baringa had no idea why Bolder had attacked him, and no further interest in him. His enormous problem was how to find Dawn. So Baringa, stiff, and blood-stained, and exhausted, went off quietly through thick snowgums and tea-tree, crossed the Limestone with great care, and, keeping to the teatree, went down the west side of the river. He did not see Yarolala, half-asleep on the ground.

When he had gone a mile or so he slid into a dense thicket and rested until he could start his search at daylight.

Once he started off, he combed the bush from side to side, leaving no yard of the river bank unsearched, examining it for track or strand of silver hair: going inland, too, peering into snowgrass glades where she might have gone to rest: seeking out the hidden places among rocks into which a mare might go to give birth to her foal.

Never a trace or track did he find – no hair entangled in a teatree limb, no hoof mark pressed into a wombat track. The rain that began to fall worried him because it would wash away all marks. When the rain changed to snow, his eyelashes were clogged with it, and it matted his mane, lay on his back, stinging all the kicks and bites which Bolder had given him, making them ache, but he only thought of Dawn, wondering whether this cold snow fell on her.

On and on he went, resting at night because he had to have daylight. He passed below the place where Dawn had fallen into the creek, and intensified his search. Near here he did find fresh hoof marks, and could tell that there were a pair of young stallions and three or four fillies. He followed their tracks, but he felt certain, after a while, that even though their tracks were always all muddled up together, Dawn's was never there. He thought he might find the little herd and ask if they had seen any sign of her, so he followed on and on, but went a long way without finding them.

To and fro, back and forth, he searched, often calling, because he did not care who heard him. The warm sun had come through again. He saw a hanging curtain of sarsaparilla bursting into bloom, and there was the liquid song of the thrush in the air, rising high above the sound of the river. Baringa felt his step growing light in time with the spring. Dawn was his. Soon he *must* find her.

He had passed the mouth of the Tin Mine Creek, coming in on the opposite side, bringing the water from Dale's Creek too. It swelled the river even wider and deeper. Ahead, a creek came in on this west side, and the water made a great noise.

The sun had set behind Davies Plain, and all the light was red-gold when Baringa stood on the bank of this deep-flowing, narrow creek. He thought he would have to go upstream in order to cross it.

Partly because of the lovely spring evening, but also with the never-dying hope that he would get an answer, Baringa stood on the deep-cut bank and called as loudly as he could, so that his neigh might sound over the roar of the stream.

He had thrown his head right up, and noticed a great lot of kurrawongs high in the glowing sky. He could not hear their song above the water's roar, so how could he expect his call to be heard? How could he expect to hear an answer?

Then all of a sudden, as he stood, still trembling from all the effort of his tremendous neigh, he heard something ... something blending in with the sound of the stream. Could it be an answer? Could it be Dawn? And where, exactly, did the sound come from?

With his head still up, he called again, the whole of his immensely strong silver body quivering with the effort to throw his call far above the noise of the water.

Then he waited.

It was impossible to be certain that he heard an answering neigh, yet surely he had. He moved upstream and called again. This time he could not hear anything. He would try to cross ... but crossing was going to be difficult – the creek was so narrow, so deep, and so extremely swift. As he went further up the creek he kept on calling.

After a while he saw that what he had thought was the opposite bank was in fact an island. The stream was broader above, and split by the island.

He swam across the broader, less swift part of the stream. Even that was a struggle, because it was a very deep creek, full of snow water, and in it were a few massive boulders or rock ribs that twisted his legs. He climbed out on the far side, shook himself in a cloud of glittering spray, and trotted down till he was opposite the island. Already the light was beginning to fade.

He threw back his head and called and called.

Yes, oh surely yes. He must have heard an answer, and it must be from the island. He called again and waited. He was not imagining it, there really was an answer.

He looked at the island. This side of it was steep and rocky. Scrub grew right to the edge of the rocks and hung over towards the water. The other side would be better to get on to – if either side were good.

He called and called. Each time he was sure he got an answer, but he saw no sign of any other horse, and there was nowhere on this side of the island where a horse could stand. He would have to go back across the stream and try from the other side.

As he trotted back upstream he turned and looked at the topmost part of the island, where the stream split into two. Just on the upper side of the point there was a break in the rocks, a possible place to land, if the water did not sweep him past it, and a possible opening in the rocks through which to scramble up on to the island.

He gave another neigh, but this time could hear nothing. However, he was certain that some answer had come from the island.

He went a little further up the creek before going into the water, to be sure to give himself time to swim out of the main current that flowed down past the island and into the big river.

Then, rather slowly, and watching the water to see which way the strongest eddies went, he slithered down into the freezing stream.

This time he had to swim very hard to get out of the main current. The force of the water and the cold drove the breath out of him. He swam with all his strength, feeling all the cuts of the fight aching in the bitter cold. He was being raced down by the water at a terrific speed. He struggled furiously to get out of the current, only his cream and silver head showing above the muddy water. Then suddenly he was being hurtled towards the island at such a rate that he felt sure he would smash his bones if he hit the rocks full force.

He made a last tremendous effort to steer himself to the one place where he could land. All at once he felt sand under his hooves. His quarters, in deeper water, were being swung round, but he managed to pull himself forward and upwards. With a great leap, he was standing breathless in a tiny niche between rocks, shivering with cold and effort.

He pushed a way through rocks and teatree. A branch scraped one of his bites and made it bleed again.

The teatree was very thick. At last he came to a flat-topped rock on which he could stand clear of the suffocating leaves and twigs. There he stopped and called.

From quite close came the answering cry.

"Here am I."

Baringa's heart gave a thudding bound within his deep, silver chest. He was right. Dawn was alive. He leapt through the teatree, pushing it out of his way, calling and calling as he went, barely waiting for the answer.

He burst through the bush into an unexpected clearing, and there, in the middle, stood Dawn, a little silver colt, trembling with fear, standing pressed against her flanks.

Baringa was overjoyed. He propped to a standstill and just gazed. It was Dawn, Dawn who had loved him so dearly ever since he was only a yearling, who came forward, leading his little son.

99

As soon as her sweet, soft nose touched his, he felt warmth flood through him. For all his courage in holding to the belief that she must live, Baringa had, like Benni, been very afraid for a mare in that flood, a mare so soon to foal.

"I knew you would find us," Dawn said. "I cannot get off this island with the foal, but there has been grass and leaves enough for me to eat. The foal was very weak, but he is stronger now." She began to nuzzle Baringa all over, to warm him after the freezing stream, then she led him to a patch of sand in which to roll so that he got dry. She could not stop doing little dancing steps all around him.

The foal became more confident, watching his mother nuzzling the great horse.

That night the foal slept at his mother's feet, beneath an overhanging rock. She and Baringa stood flank and flank, the warmth flowing from one to another.

Baringa gradually learnt all that had happened since she had heard his last despairing cry on that dark evening, as she was swept down the river.

Dawn had been almost unconscious with cold, and had felt deeply that she was going to drown, when suddenly there were trees looming beside her, and she had felt ground beneath her hooves. It had been an enormous effort to hold on and scramble out. If she had not been washed against a log, she might never have succeeded in getting right out, but the log stopped the current sweeping her off the island to which fortunately, it had taken her.

She had collapsed at the edge of the water and then felt the flood coming higher. The freezing cold, as the water lapped up around her legs, had made her get up and go inland to the grass glade, which was then more mud than grass, and even one patch of snow still remained. There, some hours later, her foal was born.

Both she and the foal had been very weak for some days, but the warmth of the sun and the spring growth had helped them, and now they were much better, in fact Baringa knew that Dawn had looked more beautiful than ever, when he saw her standing there, in the glade, with her foal.

They slept the night in great happiness. In the morning

Baringa was awoken by the hungry foal stumbling to its feet and seeking its mother's milk.

Baringa yawned contentedly, and rested his neck over Dawn's. As the light came he could see that her coat was indeed shining, that she gleamed all over.

It was not till the sun was well up that he began to wander round the island ... began to wonder how he was going to get Dawn and the foal off.

The front of the island, where Dawn had landed, would be the only place where they could get the foal into the water, he knew, so he pushed his way through the teatree to have a look.

For the first time, the idea sank into him that it might be very difficult to get the foal away till the river dropped a great deal. In his efforts to get on to the island, he had simply never given a thought to the problem of leaving it again. He had only thought of finding Dawn, and though he had known that the fact that she was going to have a foal was the main hazard in her being swept away by the flood, he had not thought of finding her with a foal at foot – not thought of the complications that would make as regards getting back to the Canyon.

He walked into the water from the front of the island. No current pulled and tugged just there. He went in as far as he could go without swimming, but he could see that there was no possibility of getting away without going into the main river. He walked back on to dry land, shook himself in the hot sunshine, went back through the teatree and played with Dawn and the foal.

In this weather the river must drop.

Each day Baringa went to look at the river. He could see the flood level on the rocks and knew the water was dropping and dropping. At last he thought that he must go out into the river, himself, to see where the current would take him. He warned Dawn that he would be away for some time.

Her soft blue and brown eyes filled with fear, though she knew they must go back, and also knew that the food on the island was not sufficient.

"The foal will be so afraid," she said. "He is so small, and he is not strong like Dilkara was. He had too hard a time."

101

"Wait till I see how the river is," Baringa said, and went through the tunnel he had made in the teatree.

He stepped into the water again, walking in deeper and deeper, hating the iron bands of cold. He started to swim, but only just enough to keep himself afloat, so that he would have an idea what would happen to the foal, when it got in. He floated along, finding that he was being taken quite fast towards the eastern bank of the river. Provided the landing place was all right, they might get the foal across.

There was what looked like a good, shelving bank ahead, and the curve of a ridge to stop any of them being washed further. Already quite a lot of logs had been dropped by the flood on that ridge.

Baringa landed safely and without much trouble. He immediately began to trot upstream, and went quite a distance. When he had rolled, bucked, reared and rolled again to warm himself, he sprang into the river again, and struck out as hard as he could. To get back across to the western bank was not quite so easy, and he was very cold when he landed. He still had to swim the creek to the island.

He got there safely and it was very pleasant to roll in the sandy patch on the island, and to have Dawn with whom to romp and play till he was warm and dry. The spring sun beat down on them, filling them with vigour. Even the foal joined in the play.

"We should name him for the flood," said Baringa.

"No," answered Dawn, "nothing terrible like that. Name him for the marvellous beauty of the frost on snow. Let him be called Kalina."

When Baringa tried to get Dawn to take Kalina to the river she would not move. Baringa gave in, because he thought Dawn should know, but when clouds started rolling up, he began to wonder how wise he had been, not to persuade her to come. If much rain fell, the river would rise once more.

"Let us go," he said. "It will rain again," but she insisted on staying a few more days for her foal to grow stronger.

So that wild thunder storm which had shown Lightning the dead dun, and through which he and Thowra had travelled to Quambat, through which Yarolala had taken herself to see if Baringa were alive or dead, lighted up Baringa and Dawn and their foal on the tiny island. The teatree was silvered by the flashing light, Kalina neighed with fear and Dawn comforted him. Once she saw Baringa stand on a rock as though welcoming the great noise and the vivid light, as though he were part of the vast storm and its strength. And, in that flash, Dawn saw him as a magnificent mature stallion, one who should be free to roam wherever he wished, unafraid of any other horse. She knew it was time they should leave the island, and that her little foal, son of Baringa, should somehow have the strength to swim.

The rain that came after the storm made Baringa fear for a rise in the river, but in fact the water did not rise much, and the rain did not fall for long.

After the sun came out again, and they were playing in the glade, Baringa noticed that Kalina's games were more vigorous, that indeed he must be strengthening.

The time to try to move had come. After one more day he led Dawn and their son through his teatree tunnel. There was a sandy beach now, at the edge of the water, an encouraging place from which to step off.

Baringa went in first. Kalina watched trembling, but when

103

his mother went in, he raced about on the beach, neighing with fear.

Dawn called him quietly. After a while he calmed down and walked in, fetlock-deep, but scrambled out again. Dawn went back for him. Eventually he walked in beside her.

Baringa watched anxiously. He saw them swimming, then he struck out into the current and they followed, the small silver head beside Dawn's.

With the stallion and the mare trying to protect the foal from the force of the current, the three of them sailed downstream to the shelving bank where Baringa had landed, and there they climbed out of the water to safety. They found sand for rolling, they raced and played, Dawn and Baringa so relieved to have Kalina safely across that they sprang around like foals themselves.

In the warm sunshine they played all the way up to the mouth of the Tin Mine Creek. There, on the long tongue of land where they had spent much of the heavy winter, they slept the night – the same night on which the black stallion moved round and round on Quambat Flat, the night which Thowra spent not very far away from them, inland on the other side of the river: the night Yarolala, and the emus, and Lightning too, all hid in different patches of trees around Quambat Flat.

The foal seemed none the worse for his freezing swim, and next morning Baringa led the two up the Tin Mine Creek. He was uncertain how the foal would climb round all those cliffs, so when the gorge began to narrow, he led them up on to the hillside behind the cliffs. It meant a longer journey – right round the whole Tin Mine Gorge, into the gentler valley behind, then over the ridge and down into the Canyon – but he was sure of Kalina being able to climb by that route.

When they had climbed up, high above the trees, on to a clear, rocky area, Baringa stood on the furthest jutting-out rock – one which was just touched by the early sunlight – and called out a joyous call to the world.

Suddenly there was an answer, faint and clear, from far below. Baringa reared with joy and flung out his call to Thowra:

"All is well, is well!" and back came the echoing answer.

104

Knowing that Thowra must have been searching for him and for Dawn, and that he would now know that he need search no longer, Baringa went on very happily.

They rested the foal often, up that steep mountain, so it took more than half the day to climb it. When they reached the valley of the Tin Mine, the foal was very tired, and though Baringa and Dawn were both longing to go on, right to the Canyon to see the others, they knew they should rest for the night where they were, where the grass was sweet and tender, and Kalina could sleep.

Dawn, thinking how Baringa had looked in the flash of lightning – a splendid stallion – had thought several times since, that a horse such as he should have quite a herd. She found out that he had been far too worried about her to take time to collect even the round mare who belonged to the black stallion. There would be time, now, she thought, and he would be able to take his herd with him, all over the southern mountains, for Baringa would be unbeatable.

Dreaming happily, she slept beside Baringa and her foal, there on the Tin Mine Creek, till the stars started to pale, and it was time to go up the ridge and then down the great, steep side of the Canyon.

Thirteen

Dawn woke Kalina and made him have a drink before they moved on their way to the Canyon. She stood placidly while the foal sucked. Though she was looking forward to getting back, looking forward to showing her foal to Moon and Koora, she was so happy to be with Baringa again that nothing else, except the well-being of the foal, really seemed to matter.

Baringa, knowing that Benni had felt sure that Dawn must be drowned – though not knowing the rumour that he, himself, was dead – was more anxious to get her safely home, but he, too, was so happy that he did not mind for how long the foal sucked. He did hope that it would not get so full that it wanted to sleep. So he stood with one eye partly shut, half-dreaming,

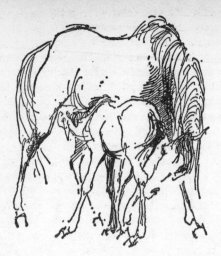

seeing himself leading Dawn and their foal off the path by the bluff, towards Moon, dreaming of Benni's delight.

At last Dawn thought the little colt had had enough, and she started to move through the trees where they had slept. Then Baringa took the lead and they went steeply upwards on the last ridge dividing them from the Canyon. On the other fall of this ridge were the great, precipitous, tree-clad slopes and the cliffs – and Benni, Moon and Koora waiting.

The sun warmed them all the way up. On the top of the ridge it was cooler because of the space around them and the huge depth of the Canyon. The foal ran along beside Dawn, occasionally bumping into her. When they reached the edge, Baringa stood looking over, a faint breeze lifting his mane and forelock. Kalina stood beside him, and Dawn watched the breeze ruffle the shaggy fur of mane on the little horse.

They stepped down and out of the warm sunlight, the foal apparently unafraid of the steepness, so that Dawn wondered if he would always have some fear of water, and yet be fearless of everything else.

Going down this way, they would not see into the Canyon much before they got there, so they were almost all the way down when they saw the creek and some of the green grass ... and Benni and Silky hopping out of the trees ... and

Moon . . . and Koora with Dilkara . . . and . . .

Baringa stopped in astonishment.

Dawn felt the feeling of horror go through him, seconds before she saw what had caused it. Then she let the air through her nostrils noiselessly, in a half-amused snort, because, following Dilkara, as though she had not a care, was a little, pert, round, white mare.

"Why are you so worried?" she said into Baringa's twitching ear.

"She belongs to the black stallion," Baringa answered. "He may be here, too. Wait, and I shall go and see."

"We will come," Dawn announced. "There is no stallion in the mountains for you to fear now."

Baringa looked at her, then, saying no more, started to walk on.

He stopped again! This time Dawn's snort of amusement could be heard.

Behind the pert, white mare came a beautiful pale blue roan filly, very like Koora.

"Some stallion must have come here," muttered Baringa, his neck arched, his nostrils dilated. And on he went, into the Canyon.

Benni and the herd had filed past and gone upstream a little way, without there being any sign of another stallion. Baringa stopped again. If there were no stallion, how had the mare and filly found his Canyon? He looked round at Dawn and saw a gleam of amusement in her eye.

Then he whinnied, not loud enough to be heard beyond the Canyon. Every animal swung round, and Benni, with great rhythmic bounds, came racing towards him. Even the shy and nervous Moon was cantering, either to him or to Dawn. Then a soft paw patted his nose in passing, as the little kangaroo hopped to Dawn, put his paws up to her muzzle, giving short barks of delight.

Definitely there was no other stallion. Baringa could greet Moon and Koora – could wait a moment or so before asking what he greatly wished to know.

The blue filly and the round, white mare were looking at each other and then at the group below the cliff. . . . Thowra

107

had said "the most beautiful stallion in all the mountains," and they had both thought Thowra more handsome than any horse they had ever seen, but now ... this horse was younger ... he was Thowra again, and yet he was not. ... They waited.

At last Benni turned his attention to Baringa. Baringa had never seen his old friend so overjoyed. He caught one soft grey paw between his lips, teasing, and Benni patted him with the other paw.

"Did you think you were going to have to look after Moon for ever, Benni?" he asked gently.

"Your grandsire and I were both afraid," Benni answered, "but we have forgotten! Thowra thought that the lovely mares he brought you must help bring you home!" Benni scratched one ear with a strangely comical expression on his pointed face.

Baringa heard Dawn's amused snort again.

In Baringa's own eyes, as he looked at the mares again, there was a gleam of laughter.

It was Benni who really knew of the desperate fear in Thowra's heart which could only be assuaged by doing something that would somehow make it be that Baringa was alive. He wondered where Thowra was now because the sooner the Silver Stallion knew that Baringa and Dawn were safe, the better. More mares would fill the Canyon to overflowing!

As though answering his thought, Baringa said:

"Thowra knows that we were on our way home. He heard me call, and answered from the other side of the river."

"Ahh," Benni said, and then gave a violent sneeze, for here the wattles were only just coming into full bloom.

Koora and Moon were gently sniffing the foal whom Dawn proudly showed off to them. Baringa turned his attention to the blue filly and the round white one. He walked proudly across the grass towards them. Even the black stallion's pert mare stood with her head up, nose trembling, ears flickering, as Baringa went to greet them.

Baringa could not help wondering, during that sunny day, how Thowra got that pert, white mare from the black, and how his Canyon would hold them all. They would look beautiful grazing and playing on the green grass of Quambat Flat.

That morning Yarolala was still in the trees beside Quambat Flat, watching the black stallion seeking tracks of his roans that would lead him to where they were now. She, herself, could only wish for the scent and spoor of Baringa.

All at once the black must have found tracks that actually led somewhere and were not just made by the herd when grazing. He set off in a purposeful way, following them. Yarolala watched closely – and was sure she saw a movement among the trees near the black – a light-coloured movement. Lightning must be shadowing him, and what would Lightning do?

Just then Yarolala felt as though a cloud had gone over the sun, cold all down the back, cold with fear. There had been a sound in the trees near her. She was afraid to move, afraid even to turn her head in case she made herself noticeable.

She looked sideways, rolling her eyes as far as she could. Something was moving in the bush ... something. . . . Then Yarolala saw feathers swaying and bouncing. She turned noiselessly to face the emus. These emus pretended they knew everything – perhaps they did know where Baringa hid his mares. . . . To be as polite as possible, she walked towards them, and bowed her head ceremoniously.

"Hail Yarolala," the birds said. "What are you doing, hidden here? When we last saw you, you had joined Lightning's herd. Perhaps you are wise to leave them again. There is going to be trouble!"

"Greetings, O emus. I have not left just because there was going to be trouble. I left some days ago. I beg you once more to tell me where Baringa runs. I most deeply need the help of all your wisdom."

The emus looked at her piercingly. They had made some investigations since she had first asked this question which had caused them to become aware that there was indeed a mystery about Baringa, and they had learnt a little. Also they had heard of her report that Baringa was dead, and there was, after that, the added puzzle of a blue filly being with Thowra one day and having vanished the next, and the rumour that the same thing had happened to the round, white mare.

Neither emu spoke for a moment or so, then the male said: "A secret is a secret."

109

"Baringa's secret will remain untold if I find him," Yarolala said proudly.

"Even if he did not want to share his secret? Even if he never wants more than his mares who are like the sun and the moon to him?"

Yarolala shivered.

"I will never tell his secret," she answered.

"And what if he really is dead? You told Lightning that you saw him die."

"His body no longer lies there," Yarolala answered. "Neither he nor Bolder lie there. I saw the glade empty, as the lightning flashed. I walked over to where they had lain. There were no dead horses."

"It is not for us to tell Baringa's secret," the emu said. "Seek! Try Dale's Creek again, though it is a place of danger. Now we go to see how Lightning fares. The black is the stronger horse." The emus started to walk away, but they watched Yarolala to see if she was in any way bothered about what happened to Lightning. They had no wish to cause real trouble by giving her a hint how to find Baringa, if she might return to Lightning's herd. But Yarolala was already moving off through the trees towards the Pilot Gap and Dale's Creek.

Yarolala walked carefully, but the sun was warm, the birds were singing and wattles scented the air. Baringa was alive! She was young and she was beautiful. Occasionally she did a few little dancing steps for joy. Somehow she must find him and never lose him again.

She crossed over the Pilot Gap and began to drop down into the head of Dale's Creek. An unknown horse flitting through the trees gave her a fright. She tried to hide herself with more care. She wondered if the emus did know where Baringa hid, or were they just pretending, and sending her on a wild goose chase? She did not really think so, because Dale's Creek was about the only place left in which his hiding place could be. She kept remembering the scent of Baringa on the Quambat Ridge. From where had he come then?

She was glad when she got into the teatree on the valley floor. It was more comfortable to be hidden. With every step she grew more and more nervous, but she was determined. Whatever fear she felt, she must go on and on till she found

110

Baringa. She examined every sandy patch that she came to, but there seemed to be no fresh tracks. The gaiety had gone out of her step. She was alone, and having to draw up her courage. A kookaburra's sudden laughter made her sweat with fright. She stood for a moment in a thick clump of teatree till her trembling grew quieter.

She had gone a long way down the creek, and still there was no sign of a hiding place. She did not think she could have missed anything, but of course, to be any good, a hiding place must be difficult to find. She half wondered if she had missed a gorge cutting back into the Quambat Ridge.

Everything was so silent. At Quambat or on the Ingegoodbee one heard the sound of other horses. Here even the call of the birds seemed muted. Yarolala felt her coat creeping as she walked on.

The more afraid she became, the prouder she looked, so that the spirit of Yarraman walked through the eerily silent bush, and the sunlight flashed on her silver mane and tail, which were also Yarraman's, made living gold of her hide as it had his hide, in the Cascades, years ago.

If only she had seen a wombat or a kangaroo, the valley would not have seemed so lonely. She kept thinking of Baringa, and the vision of him rose in her mind – the silver horse, lighter in build than Thowra because he was younger, yet so like him, all fire and eagerness, and still noble and gentle. She almost expected to see him coming towards her with his proud, swinging stride, but the valley was empty.

The creek curved a little westward, and there the character of the valley changed. Instead of being open, with snowgrass and teatree flats, it narrowed between swiftly steepening ridges. There were rocks ahead, Yarolala could see. She still kept herself in the thick teatree, but there was an open stretch. She stopped and peered through the leaves. All was quiet. She stepped out of her cover, went forward a few yards towards the rock ribs that came right to the creek. Then she went cold all over, and backed hastily into the teatree.

What was it lying in the water? Undoubtedly a horse. She turned round and pushed quickly through the trees. She could not pass close to that dead horse, and there was no way of getting to the rocks without passing fairly close to it.

111

She stopped in the thick teatree, her heart pounding. She would climb up on to the side of the High Plateau. Perhaps she might get round the rocks far above, might see what lay beyond. Something must.... She had seen a place from the High Plateau which she thought no horse could get into.... So she turned and climbed.

When she began to edge over so that she would pass above the rocks, the hillside was a lot steeper. It was difficult to climb, very difficult not to slide. She kept on for quite a way, sweating and panting. When she tried to go downwards, thinking she must have passed over the top of the rocks, she found herself sliding on her haunches and quite unable to stop. Luckily she slid, chest on, into a tree, and managed to get to her feet again.

She tried to go back the way she had come, climbing higher, rather than going downwards, which was so slippery. And as she climbed she wondered if there could be some deep hole in the hills, below her, part of which she had seen from the High Plateau. Except by passing the dead horse, she did not know how she would reach it.

She would have to gather up her courage and pass that horse, and Yarolala had been gathering her courage for so long now.

At last, without falling again, she arrived on a gentler slope above Dale's Creek.

The sun had long since slid down behind the High Plateau when she got back on to the banks of the creek, and bars of light filtered through the trees. Everything was tinged cold green and seemed fluid, unreal.

Then, in that queer, flowing green light, she saw the dead horse again. It would have to be passed. She held herself tense, and began walking along the bank, eyes and nostrils dilated, flesh trembling. Soon she was near enough to see that the horse had been dead for several days and then with another jolt of horror, she realised that it was the dun stallion who had left Quambat Flat to try to find Baringa's mares. She was trembling like a snowgum leaf in the wind.

Who had killed the dun horse? Who? Who?

She forced herself to keep walking. Soon she was at the rocks and scrambling up on to them. The light was becoming

112

dimmer, which was perhaps lucky, because there was no cover.

What was that? A movement ahead? That rock had moved, or was it a stump?

"Yarolala," a voice said softly. "What are you seeking?" and the stump had become a grey kangaroo with ears pricked, paws folded in front.

Yarolala's heart was thundering. She could barely get her breath at all, but she remembered having seen this kangaroo once, with her own sire.

"O kangaroo," she said. "I have seen you speaking with my sire, Son of Storm, and I have heard how the birds and animals of the bush are friends of the Silver Herd's, so I will answer your question. I seek Baringa."

"Why do you seek him here?"

"Partly because I feel his hiding place must be somewhere near here, partly because the emus suggested I should try Dale's Creek."

"Why is it that you seek him at all?"

"Because he is the most beautiful horse in the mountains."

"Have you the courage to wait here, hidden in teatree without moving for quite a long time?"

"Yes," she answered.

"Well, hide yourself, so that I know you are hidden before I go. I will come back."

Yarolala, sidling away from the dead horse and barely looking at it, walked back to the teatree. When he was satisfied that she was properly hidden, Benni went leaping off through the twilight.

Yarolala had to wait a long time, near the dead horse, and it took all her courage, and all her desperate love for Baringa. Night came, filling the valley, and the sounds of the night seemed eerier, lonelier than usual. She was starting to feel very afraid, when Benni came back.

"Yarolala," he whispered. "Come out." And there was a scent on the night air, thrilling, lovely.

She stepped out. In the darkness she could just see the shadow form of a silver horse.

"Baringa!" she almost cried his name aloud. Benni tapped her swiftly on the nose to silence her.

"Yarolala," Baringa said. "Why have you left Lightning?"

113

"I followed your scent the night you fought Bolder, and saw you fight. I thought you were both dead, so I went back to Quambat. Then, later, I went to see if you really had died, and I have been searching for you since."

"I see," said Baringa. "Did you tell them at Quambat that I had died?"

"Yes, I did."

"And now do they know that you did not find my body?"

"No, but the emus may tell them."

Baringa blew gently through his nostrils, thinking how, if he believed him dead, Lightning would never rest till he found Dawn. At last he spoke again:

"Yarolala," he said. "Any mare that comes with me has to remain hidden and keep my hiding place a secret. Will you promise me this, O great-grand-daughter of Yarraman?"

"I promise you faithfully."

So Baringa led her up the ridge, away a little from the dead dun, on a way he knew through the rocks. Yarolala was so happy to be following him at last that she barely noticed his horrified appearance as he looked down on the heap that had once been a horse, lying down in the creek.

She put her feet exactly where he put his feet, moved in time with his movements, went through the bush with Baringa, belonging to him. Benni, looking pleased, bounded rhythmically alongside.

Baringa paused before the steepest part of the descent.

"Where is Lightning now?" he asked.

"Lightning!" Yarolala was thinking of no one except Baringa, and she was so happy that she had forgotten the black stallion, forgotten Lightning. "Why, Lightning," she went on. "He's probably still fighting the black stallion over those roan mares."

"The black is there!"

"Yes. He spent a whole night prowling round the flat, trying to find tracks that would lead him to wherever Lightning had taken his roans. He had just discovered their spoor and was heading for the Cobras when I left the trees where I had been standing watching."

"So they had not started to fight?"

"No."

114

Baringa said no more, and led down into the Canyon.

The night was only lit by the stars, but the three white mares and the two pale roans, the silver yearling and the silver foal, all took shape in starlight. Yarolala looked at them rather shyly. She was not silver, but she was of the Yarraman blood, as Baringa was too. Then she recognised the black stallion's round, white mare, and was amazed.

Benni and Silky, invisible in the night, looked at the mares and thought they were a most beautiful herd.

Fourteen

When Yarolala left Quambat she had been right in thinking that Lightning was shadowing the black, but as soon as Lightning was certain that the other stallion had indeed picked up the tracks of his roan mares, and was going to follow them, he took a short cut so that he might reach the mares first and possibly be able to get them away and hide them.

Unfortunately the black went far faster than he expected. Lightning had only just arrived near his mares when he heard a trumpeting snort, and the black was almost upon them.

The black horse saw his own roans and was just starting towards them, without even realising Lightning was there, when suddenly it was as though he saw Goonda for the first time. He stopped with one forefoot raised, and simply stared at her. Then he began to walk slowly, proudly, towards her.

In that moment Lightning learnt one thing. He learnt that even the remembered beauty of Dawn meant nothing to him compared with his feeling for Goonda. He bounded forward, between the black and his red roan mare – and in the swiftness of his movements, his courage, and his fire, he suddenly looked far more like his sire, Thowra.

Even the black paused for a second as he saw Lightning coming, for Lightning's quality was such that one might pause, also this was surely not the horse whom he had seen once blood-stained and exhausted – seen and then lost? The second's pause gave Lightning time to hurl himself at him.

Even with that first crashing impact, Lightning knew that this was the strongest, heaviest horse he had ever fought, knew that, if he were to survive, he would have to alter his method of fighting to something more like Thowra's and Baringa's strike-and-leap-away, bite-and-dodge tactics. His only hope, Lightning was sure, was to exhaust this horse.

Goonda did the most sensible thing possible. She led her foal, now nearly a yearling, and Steel's grey mares off towards Cloud. The five roans belonging to the black did not want to go with her, so she left them to follow the queer running fight that began to develop. However, the fight, too, went in that direction, because the black saw Goonda going that way and he was determined not to lose sight of her.

Lightning was equally determined that he would not let the black get her, but he was very frightened because of the black's greater strength. For the first time Lightning felt that he would give his life to protect someone else, and that he would surely rather die than lose Goonda.

Somehow the great strength of this feeling gave him an endurance and a speed which he had never before possessed.

For a while the black stallion simply tried to defeat Lightning, probably thinking that it would be fairly easy, and that, once he had defeated the silver horse, he would be able to take his own mares and this beautiful light-red one, with the spirited, intelligent head, the tossing mane and tail of red and silver.

Lightning, however, managed to dodge and strike, leap and kick, so cleverly that the black soon began to think that it might be more profitable to try to take the lovely mare and thus turn Lightning into the attacker – he might then be more easily beaten.

Their fighting had taken them only a little distance along the flat. Now the black set off at a gallop towards where Goonda, seeming on fire with life, stood near Cloud, and Mist, and Cirrus.

Lightning sprang after him, and very soon was cutting across him, crashing into his shoulder. The shock made them both recoil, but the black was not easily put off, and instead of attacking again, as Lightning had hoped he would, he just gathered himself together and galloped on.

Lightning had to go faster than he had ever gone before to try to catch him. He could see Goonda partly behind Cloud. She was looking anxious. Lightning hurled himself at the black horse. His teeth fastened into flesh – and held. One foreleg went between the black's forelegs. The sky and the trees began to sail past, and the warm, green grass of Quambat Flat was rushing upwards, as they fell. The black horse would be able to get up first; he was on top. Lightning shut his teeth like a clamp and held on with every ounce of strength and determination that he could muster.

They began to roll over, a kicking, struggling mass of cream and black, silver mane and tail flying with black mane and tail; and the black stallion was screaming with anger.

Lightning knew he would not be able to hold on for ever. He succeeded in getting his legs and feet underneath him just as he felt his jaws slipping. He was up as quickly as the black. He made a tremendous effort to reach Goonda first, and to stand between her and the advancing stallion.

Goonda gave a little whinny of encouragement. Goonda, who had left Whiteface's herd to go with Lightning when they were only two-year-olds, and who had been with him ever since, knew Lightning as well as any horse or mare did, and she had recognised the new quality in him, recognised with joy that it had been called up by his desire to protect her, by his desperate fear of losing her. To Goonda, Lightning had always been handsome, now, all at once and for her, he was vital with the undefeatable spirit that burnt in Thowra and in Baringa.

Goonda could see that the black horse was the stronger, but she felt a certainty that Lightning's new spirit could hold him against the other's physical strength so that he would not be beaten. She wondered should she and her yearling slide away unseen, and try to hide in the rocks on the Cobras, the only hiding place being right near the top, but she wanted so deeply to watch Lightning – this new Lightning who seemed to have grown in quality because of her.

Cloud was watching too.

Scent of spring enveloped them, scent of wattles, warm in the sunshine. This was the season for fighting among stallions.

117

Tragedy sometimes came, but life and youth took over, foals were begotten, and those begotten last year were born. The world re-created itself in the spring, and creation was joy – though of course the spring was not joy for those who had their mares stolen, or who were hurt and maimed in the fights. But life went on.

Goonda knew she would belong to Lightning for ever.

The black horse was charging Lightning. He was upon him, hooves flailing, and Lightning could not jump aside this time, because Goonda was behind him.

Amazed, Goonda watched him move slightly, and so lightly, rear up and crash his forefeet down on the advancing stallion. Lightning was fighting a magnificent fight, but the black succeeded in getting in the hardest blows.

It would give Lightning a better chance to dodge, Goonda thought, if she moved away. She backed into the trees and moved off quietly.

Lightning felt her going, and started to leap and tease, just the same way as he had seen Thowra and Baringa do.

The black realised she had moved, and could not see which way she had gone. Goonda, looking round as she walked, nearly bumped into the emus, but, except to give them a polite greeting, she said nothing.

She could not bear to go completely out of sight of the fight, so she walked a short distance through the trees and then got herself to where she could see out without being seen.

Lightning was still successfully dodging, and leaping in occasionally with a strike or bite.

The black's five roans were standing at the edge of the bush. Goonda wondered if they would come if she called them. Their sudden vanishing from sight might upset the black.

She called quietly. The roans lifted their heads. She called again; they began to move towards her. Goonda waited till they got close, then she moved silently through the bush, and called from a little further off.

"Come, quick, quick!"

The black did not miss the mares for quite a while, and when he did, he let his attention wander, and received, on

118

his off hip, the first really heavy blow that Lightning had
managed to land on him. The black shook himself, but went
rushing off to find his roans. The roans were his. They must
stand near, so he could see them.

Lightning chased him.

Slowly the day wore on. The two horses were streaked
with sweat, tired and thirsty. Both were stiffening slightly,
the black from the blow on the hip, and it looked as though
he might be the stiffest the next day. At last he began to
retreat for the night, backing away towards the roans. Lightning was so tired that he did not follow immediately, but
joined Goonda, got a drink, had some grass.

There would be a faint new moon that night. Perhaps when
night came ... But of course Lightning was visible by night,
and the black almost invisible.

Lightning did not desperately mind whether he lost the
roans or not – Goonda was the one who mattered – but still
it might be better to try to take them back during the night.
It might, of course, be better to rest.

All round the flat there were movements and sounds. Horses
had come down from Forest Hill, from the Cobras, to see
what was going on, and the bush birds and animals that might
ordinarily have gone further afield as night came, stayed in
the trees nearby – or came closer.

119

Leaves and branches moved, shrubs rustled. There was a faint twittering. Small, bright eyes peered through the darkness. Nothing must be missed, for two of the strongest stallions of the mountains had fought all day and only succeeded in exhausting each other.

Among all the bush birds the animals, two questions were whispered: "Where was Thowra?" "Was it true that Baringa was dead?"

If Baringa were dead, then the winner of this fight would be the greatest stallion of the south.

The black . . . the black . . . Every bird knew that the black was a fierce, strong fighter, but what was it that the kurrawongs had cried, far up in the sky? "Lightning fights as though possessed by the spirit of Thowra . . . he fights for the beautiful Goonda. . . . He will fight on and on."

The silver sickle of moon was in the sky, but shed very little light. Lightning roamed around the flat, inviting further battle, but the black did not move.

Lightning thought he would try a soft call to those roan mares and see what happened.

"Come, come away with me," he called, making his voice as gentle and as honey-sweet as he could. "Come away, come away."

The roans stirred restlessly. The first one to throw up her head with some eagerness, earned herself a sharp bite. Another began to move off and she, too, was bitten.

Lightning could not see what was happening, only hear, and guessed that the black was in an evil mood. He was not particularly happy himself, stiffening up all over, now, and very tired, but he knew that he had never fought so well before, and he knew that, to Goonda, he was wonderful, so, in spite of his stiffness, he walked with pride.

He still had Goonda with him. He must defeat this horse and be king of all the southern mountains.

At last, that night – the same night in which Baringa took Yarolala to his Canyon – Lightning and the black both slept, slept and stiffened up.

They woke during one of the light frosts of a spring morning, feeling almost unable to trot, far less gallop and fight.

Lightning wished he felt better. For some reason he remembered, though he pushed the thought away, all the times Baringa had helped him. Well, Baringa was dead now. . . .

All the next day the black and Lightning eyed each other from a distance, both far too stiff and sore to want to attack. The other horses, the birds, and the animals of the bush stayed close to Quambat Flat, wondering what would happen between the two great stallions . . . every animal wondering . . . every animal waiting . . . and Goonda and the five roan mares wondering and waiting most of all.

Goonda would have liked to suggest that they should simply go, vanish, but she knew that this time Lightning had to stay and fight this to a finish.

One more night and then half a day – and the black seemed to feel it was time to start again. He came up the flat, stepping high, head high, snorting.

In fact he was lame.

Goonda guessed that he thought he would try himself out and see what he felt like when he was warmed up. There was something about that horse which made her wish again that she and Lightning could just go away together. It was no use wishing. It was not for Lightning to wander the mountains peacefully, with one mare. Lightning would have to have a big herd, and no other horse to question his rights. Lightning would have to conquer – if he could.

She waited uneasily.

The black apparently still felt too sore to fight for very long, and though he sparred around with Lightning for a while, he soon retreated.

The next morning clouds covered over the sky, dark and heavy. The black apparently felt much better. He came up like a whirlwind, and Goonda watched, horrified. There was no mistaking his intentions: this time he meant to make a finish of the fight, meant to finish Lightning.

Lightning gave Goonda a gentle nudged towards the trees, touching his nose to hers for less than a second, and then he was walking proudly out to meet his enemy.

Goonda moved in behind some bitter pea bushes, but could not bear to go further away, as though if she were close, she could give out her strength to Lightning.

Lightning, looking quite confident, sidestepped away from

the black's first onslaught. Goonda could tell he was stiff still, but the black was still lame. Lightning wheeled round to meet the next charge, and treated it the same, except that he managed to draw blood with his teeth on the other's shoulder.

After they had danced around each other for a while, the stiffness and lameness had worn off both horses, and they were starting to sweat. Goonda could see the streaks of it beginning to stain Lightning's coat. She was sweating herself, with nervousness, and was surprised to feel a cold touch on her back, then on her rump. She looked up at the sky and saw the falling flakes.

"The snow does not want to leave the mountains this year," she thought. "Even though the hot weather is here, snow falls again. It should indeed be the year of the silver horses, for snow is theirs," and she felt cheered up by the stars and leaves of falling snow, cheered up until she thought of Baringa. . . . It had not, indeed, been his year. Goonda was fond of Baringa and she felt saddened, thinking of him. Then she wished she knew where Baringa used to hide himself and where his mares must actually be now – a hiding place could easily be useful.

Lightning was dodging the flailing hooves and the great mouth. Goonda wondered how long he would manage to keep leaping this way and that. Just then Lightning's foot slipped and the black got a grip of his neck. Goonda drew in a cold breath, a breath filled with snowflakes and with fear.

The two horses were locked together. Goonda could see that the black's grip was not a strong one and that Lightning was striking at him, fighting with all his strength.

The black stallion's grip slipped. Lightning broke free, landing a tremendous blow on the strong, black head.

For hours the fight went on, neither horse winning, but Goonda knew it was only Lightning's spirit that kept him undefeated. And the snow fell in big flakes out of the grey sky, cold on hot backs and rumps of steaming horses, cold, so cold, as it matted Goonda's mane. Slowly the ground became white. The day stretched on. Both horses were tiring, and it was now, when he was nearly exhausted, that the curtain of falling snow confused the black's judgment – or hid

Lightning sufficiently to make it difficult to strike at him accurately, so much did his cream hide, his silver mane and tail blend with the falling flakes.

Perhaps the snow saved Lightning. Just when he felt that he could dodge and strike no longer, no longer struggle, the black stallion's blows began to miss him, waste themselves on air, so that the black swung off balance, and Lightning was able to rock him further with a well-placed kick or strike.

At last the black drew away, glowering. Lightning was able to return to Goonda, and even though his flanks were heaving and his breath rasped in his throat, he could still walk with pride.

The black only rested for a short time. Then, perhaps feeling that he actually had had Lightning almost beaten, he came up the flat again, snorting and pawing the ground, throwing up the snow.

Lightning was so tired. Somehow he must go forward through the snowflakes and try, by luck, to lame or maim that black horse ... somehow ... for he was exhausted ... and tomorrow the snow might stop and he would not have the curtain of falling flakes to hide him.

Snow clung to his eyelashes, touched him cold, cold. One great blow on the black's stifle, or on a knee ... but he was so tired. . . .

He tried to strike.

The black rushed at him wildly. They were both exhausted. It was not possible to go on fighting. And the snow kept falling down out of the clouds and then out of the night sky.

Goonda rubbed her head against Lightning when he came back to her, and drew him away under some trees. Even if he would agree to go, to leave the black at his beloved Quambat Flat, he had no strength left with which to walk away ... and Goonda knew he would not leave.

In the night the snow stopped. Grey clouds were still overhead, when day broke, but during the day the clouds rolled away. Soon the sun would shine again.

The sheltering snow had gone.

The two stallions kept watchful eyes on each other. Neither had won: neither had lost. It was impossible for Lightning to drive the black from Quambat Flat; and it was impossible,

123

only just impossible for the black to take Goonda, whom he wished to have.

There, at Quambat, the silver stallion who was tired and the black one who looked thoroughly rested watched and waited.

Fifteen

Thowra, when he heard Baringa's call from across the river and high above him, had felt a sudden tremendous lightning of his spirit.

"All is well, is well," the cry had come floating down from the heights above the mouth of the Tin Mine Creek. Thowra, who was at that moment not very far from the creek that divided around the island, knew he need no longer search for Baringa, and turned up river again, light-footed with joy. He would not try to catch them up. Far better that Baringa should have the surprise of the new mares in the Canyon, without his company! He, Thowra, would seek an easy crossing place higher up, perhaps take a look in at Quambat, perhaps not, but anyway he would then go the Canyon, possibly a day after Baringa had found his increased herd. Gaily, gaily, Thowra went up the river.

Since there was no real need to plunge into that muddy, cold stream and struggle his way across it, he trotted happily upstream to the Limestone and crossed where it was shallow and easy, then he turned towards Quambat, keeping off the path and watching out for signs of the black. Having seen nothing of him, he took a look at the bare earth of the track and there, of course, were his hoof marks, also heading to Quambat.

Thowra went on, through the sunset glow, and was just at the foot of Quambat Spur, when he felt sure there was a movement in the bush, some distance off, coming from Quambat. He waited, well hidden himself, and then saw the swaying, bouncing of feathers, the rhythm of the emus' walk, before ever he could see the entire birds.

124

When they drew alongside, he moved out into the open, certainly, as he noted with some satisfaction, startling them, but his manners were so perfect, and he, himself, a horse of such importance and of such mystery, that they could not be annoyed.

"Greetings, O noble birds," he said. "Greetings, O wise and all-knowing ones. I hope you have some news for me?"

"Hail, Thowra. Of whom are you expecting news?" The birds, looking, for them, quite friendly, stared unwinkingly at him.

"Why, my son, Lightning. I observe that the black stallion is at Quambat Flat."

Surprise flitted faintly over the two sharp faces.

"Yes, he is there," they answered. "He and Lightning have not started to fight yet."

"Haven't they? Why on earth not?"

"The black has not yet seen his roan mares."

"Lightning has them hidden on the Cobras, I suppose? Is he there himself?"

"Yes, somewhere in the bush."

"Hm. Oh well, night comes soon," said Thowra. Then, as though hit by a fresh thought, he added: "I am going to the Ingegoodbee to see Son of Storm. If you are about the

125

Tin Mine track in a couple of days' time, I might hear more news from you then, before I go to Quambat Flat."

The emus nodded their heads wisely. Thowra turned into a thicket of lightwoods and sallee gums, feeling that a peaceful sleep, now that he knew Baringa and Dawn were safe, would be very pleasant, and the emus went on up the Limestone.

Thowra slept through the night, and grazed through part of the next day, then went carefully towards Quambat. He got there in time to see the last part of the first day's fighting between Lightning and the black stallion, and he watched till they drew apart, glowering at each other, neither winning, neither beaten, and he could see that the situation might remain like this for a while, so he moved on, without being seen, towards the Pilot Gap and then Dale's Creek.

Thowra kept well away from the dead dun, so he did not see any trace of Yarolala's movements, or pick up her scent, Benni's or Baringa's till he was going down the cliff, then he learnt that Baringa had taken her into the Canyon.

He walked on through the late afternoon, another proud silver horse striding down into the Canyon. There he would be greeted by his own mare, Koora. There he would greet Baringa. But first Thowra stood for a moment, looking at his grandson and all the mares, at Dawn, and her colt foal. He had felt such great anxiety for Baringa and Dawn, but now, here they were, and a lovely foal – his great-grandson. The Canyon, of course, was not large enough to hold all this herd. Baringa would have to move to Quambat and only use the Canyon if men came. But there was one thing Thowra wished to do, while the mares were still all safely hidden: he wished to take Baringa with him, back to the Secret Valley for a night and a day, provided the situation stayed the same at Quambat so that neither Lightning or the black were free to come seeking Baringa's mares. He had no doubt that the emus would bring him news along the Tin Mine track tomorrow.

In the Canyon a peaceful quiet settled down. There was the occasional snort or shuffle of hooves, but the herd slept in the stillness of the eucalypt-scented night.

The next afternoon Thowra climbed up the cliff, went

through the bush towards the Tin Mine Creek, and then got himself into the cover of some thick saplings near the track. It was not long before he saw the emus walking along with their great strides and bouncing feathers.

This time Thowra stepped quietly out on to the side of the track and walked towards them.

"Well met, O Silver Horse," the male bird said. "We have not much news for you. The black and Lightning are only looking at each other. The black has his roan mares back again, two of them being rather unwilling, and Lightning still has Goonda, though it is quite obvious that it is she whom the black wants."

"I thank you, Wise-ones," Thowra said. "I will go back now, from whence I came, and possibly return in a few days. It seems that neither the black nor Lightning can beat the other."

"The black is the stronger," the female said, "but Lightning fights with more courage than I would have expected for *him*. He fights as a son of yours really should – something he's never done before," she finished tartly.

Thowra's good manners were not quite up to answering this.

Back in the Canyon, he called Baringa. It was time they set forth together, so they climbed the cliff in the night, and headed for the Tin Mine and then the Ingegoodbee, two silver horses trotting along through darkness that was barely lit by the stars and by the faintest outline of a new moon.

When they were going down on to the head of the Ingegoodbee, Thowra thought they would go close to the huts to see if the men were there bringing cattle out yet. He and Baringa ghosted like a breath of wind down through the candlebarks till they were beside the hut. There was the smell of smoke! There was the glow, through the slab walls, of a fire, then there came the sound of men's voices. Presently there was the rattle of a chain. The tame horses must be hobbled.

Thowra and Baringa walked carefully round the outside of the fence. They could hear the sound of the hobble chains as the tame horses moved about. Apparently they did not know that the wild horses were close.

Baringa listened to them for a moment, then he called, a

sweet, quiet call beyond the hearing of men, but so thrilling and disturbing to horses:

"Come," he called, "come," and the soft call seemed to contain all the profound attraction of wild freedom – wind flowing through granite peaks, lifting mane and forelock, the gentle touch of snow, the uncommanded gallop over snow-grass – a dream that even a well-trained stock horse might never forget.

The stock horses neighed and came rattling and leaping towards them – but Baringa and Thowra had slipped away and were soon calling from the other side of the paddock.

As the hobbled horses began to neigh more wildly, the door of the hut with the fire in it opened. For a moment or so Baringa saw a man stand in the rectangle of light, heard voices clearly.

He and Thowra moved quietly away through the bush – their bush – and they went light and free, without rein or saddle.

As the hours of star-bright darkness slid past, they went over the saddle between the head of the Ingegoodbee to the Moyangul. There they found Son of Storm sleeping, disturbed him, danced and played with him, and then went on till they were in the mountain ash country, and the night wind whispered down the aisles between the towering trees, the pungent scent of the eucalypts enfolded them. On they went through the thrilling night, half-startled sometimes by the call of a mopoke or quark of a possum, and the stars shone through the tracery of eucalypt leaves high, high above them – leaf and branch making a net across the sky, but a net through which the moving stars slid as the hours passed by.

A dingo howled. Thowra neighed an answer, for what did he care if he were heard? In a few minutes they would be somewhere else. They went on eagerly.

They found Storm asleep on Stockwhip Gap, and disturbed him, so that Old Whiteface, down below, shivered in his sleep, dreaming that he heard the silver stallions. Did they, in fact, pass quite close? What caused the restless movement among his mares?

The silver horses had passed by. They were splashing, now, through Bill's Garden Creek, drinking draughts of star-marked water. They were ghosting on through the mountains – silence of silver horse, whisper of south wind to lift a silver forelock, whisper of wind through the snowgums.

They came to the cliff.

Baringa had been up it just once, when Thowra took him to the south, but he remembered it, remembered best the Lookout Platform, and he and Thowra stood there together, now, just when the first light came across from the east.

Baringa peered down into the dark valley with interest. This was his birth place: here were his mother and an unknown filly sister: here were other yearlings and foals, all related to him; here were the mares whom he could barely remember.

The fiery silver stallions walked down the faint cliff path together, and through the barely stirring darkness there came the soft rustling of hooves, then nose after nose, inquiring, sniffing gently, offering greeting. When the light came, Baringa felt that all eyes were fixed on him. He went straight to Kunama and Tambo, and did not hear the whisper:

"He is Thowra over again ... Thowra.... Baringa is Thowra...."

These mares were used to the beauty of their own stallion, yet were they deeply moved by the beauty of this young horse, so like his grandsire, but himself entirely. They remembered him as a foal and then as a spirited, but shy, yearling who went off with Thowra and Lightning, and had never returned until now.

Baringa stood in front of Kunama, his nose extended to her quivering nose, and then, coming up beside her, was an older mare, still handsome, grey and tall. It was Boon Boon who had taught all she could of wisdom to Kunama years ago, and often taught the young Baringa.

She looked at Baringa now, her eyes soft and dark with pride.

"It is fitting," she said, "that you should come back to the Secret Valley to see us once, now, when you are about to enter your kingdom."

Baringa barely heard the last words because of a thundering gallop of young horses coming to see him, but it seemed as if there was some great significance to the day, growing,

growing with each passing moment – this one day when Baringa came to see his dam and the place of his birth before – before what?

All day he grazed in the sun with Kunama, Thowra, Tambo, Boon Boon and Golden. All day the others came close for a moment and then moved on. Kunama stood beside him, sometimes her shoulder, ribs, and quarters touching his. When it was time to go, she nipped him gently on the wither.

"I named you for the swift light of the dawning," she said, "and for the sunlight that is life. Good fortune go with you, my son."

So Baringa climbed up the cliff path alone, out from the Secret Valley to trot on and on through the night till he reached his own Canyon . . . and thence to whatever the future held.

The weather was changing, he could feel the warmth in the wind, and knew that clouds were beginning to roll over the sky. When the ground permitted, he cantered. Sometimes, when there was soft snowgrass underfoot, he galloped, touched thrillingly by the night, and filled with a great excitement. His silver ears were pricked. His silver mane and tail were lifted by the wind and by his own speed through the air. . . . Powerful silver horse thrillingly possessing his own world, galloping back to his hidden, lovely herd.

So Baringa seemed almost to leap over the mountains, crossing the Moyangul, passing round the head of the Ingegoodbee, splashing through the Tin Mine Creek – till he was standing above the Canyon, then stepping down, down, down to his mares.

A current of excitement seemed to vibrate through each mare in the Canyon as he stepped down the last few feet of the cliff.

"He is here. Baringa. Baringa."

Benni hopped out of the bush. Only he and Silky of all the animals there, realised how this excitement was the same wildfire excitement that used to go wherever Thowra went – that indeed still burnt for him – and was now a leaping, crackling flame, fresh-lit for Baringa. There had only ever been one such horse in the mountains, king of all the brumbies, Thowra, the Silver Stallion. Now there was another, another silver stallion, alive with light and fire, with the spirit of the wind, some of the wisdom of the bush.

The eagles had seen this quality burning in Baringa from the sky above the Pilot, when he was still only a yearling. Benni himself had seen it. Dawn had known that there was something about the silver colt whom she had chosen.

Now was the time.

No one really slept in the Canyon that night; there was too much burning excitement. Something was going to happen. The pale, blue roan mare and the pert white mare were, at last, aware of how thrilling it was to be in Baringa's herd. Now, indeed, they knew that they belonged to the most beautiful stallion of all the southern mountains.

In the morning, with the heavy clouds pressing down and shrouding the mountain-tops, meaning something – storm or snow – Baringa asked Benni what news, if any, had come from Quambat.

"Lightning and the black are still at it. Neither can win," Benni replied, and as he spoke, the first snow-flakes began to drift through the air, falling down as though from a great height into the Canyon. Then, planing through the snow, came the eagles, low down, resting on the air above the Canyon.

Baringa enjoyed the snow. To all the silver horses it was as though snow befriended them. The horses played in the Canyon. Only Yarolala was completely visible in the drift of flakes. Baringa was without any anxiety, and his happiness sprang up in gay galloping and prancing, in hiding and in springing from invisibility to invisibility, in teasing, in loving. Only Moon was nowhere to be seen, but Dawn had assured Baringa that she would return any time, with a foal at foot.

In all his dancing, leaping games, Baringa watched for Moon, feeling certain that she would come through the snow with her foal. Until she came, the herd could not move. . . .

Late in the afternoon Baringa climbed out of the Canyon, over the bluff, and up on to the Tin Mine Track. There he watched for a while, because Thowra had said the emus might come with tidings of Quambat Flat. And through the snow they came.

131

Baringa hesitated before showing himself. While he hesitated, the bush parted and Thowra stepped out.

"Well," said Thowra. "What news, O Wise Ones?"

"They have fought again, O Thowra: and again neither has been able to win. The black is stronger and he is not exhausted. Unless anything occurs to alter things, he may beat Lightning."

Thowra said his thanks and seemed to fade away.

Baringa went back to his mares. Once again he noticed the eagles, and he rose in a half-rear to salute them as they dropped lower and lower to dip their wings.

Darkness began to seep into the Canyon, and still the snow fluttered down, and then there was a movement at the lower end of the Canyon – more solid whiteness, a sound, a soft whinny, and the frightened, high-pitched cry of the very young.

Moon came quietly walking through the snow-filled night, and a little snowy filly foal ran beside her. She was strong, Baringa noted, which was good, because soon that foal must follow the herd.

Sixteen

The light from the new moon was not bright, but it showed up the silver horse, his mares and foals, as they climbed the cliff on to the High Plateau. Sometimes they looked like formless moonbeams, and then one by one they would turn across the cliff-face on to another shelf, and all take shape, cast in glittering silver. Only Yarolala was an invisible shadow except for her mane and tail. The pale, blue-roan, daughter of Whiteface, and Koora, too, blended with the moonlight, though they did not glow in the way the silver ones did.

Up and up they climbed, closer to the moonlight and starlight. Somewhere ahead, on the High Plateau, spending the night in a great treetop, were the eagles. . . . For now was the time.

Baringa and his herd reached the top of the cliff and walked on, weaving their way through the forest – fireflies

132

or stardust, the silver horses moved in and out through the trees.

The wombats saw them, and the possums, bright-eyed in the trees watched them pass. Kangaroos saw them. Mopokes, stiff and still on their branches, watched and said nothing, for wisdom and grace, strength and courage passed below them. No brumbies knew that they were walking through the bush – not until they went down on to the gap between Dale's Creek and Quambat, and turned through the trees towards the flat.

Lightning, with Goonda, had slept the night in the trees, near the queer, sunken hole at the edge of the flat. They were still asleep and were disturbed by a slight stir of birds, the startled call of a kurrawong, the sharp pipe of a tree-creeper, and then, as though from over-flowing joy, the marvellous song of a thrush. It was not yet light. Why did the birds call? Why did the thrush sing? Lightning and Goonda became wide awake.

Something was coming through the bush like a dream. A silver horse who was said to be dead: a silver horse glowing with life, swinging along without fear of any other stallion – Baringa!

A deep sigh escaped Goonda, but Lightning simply stood and stared. Behind Baringa, following with a sort of solemn pride, was the most beautiful herd that had ever been seen in the mountains. First came Dawn, *Dawn*, and then Lightning did move, jump as though pricked by a thorn, for who was behind Dawn, was it that Hidden One? Then another white one came dancing nonchalantly along, and then Yarolala. It was when Yarolala passed that Lightning knew he was awake and not dreaming. Yarolala had told him she had seen Baringa die – and she, herself, had undoubtedly believed that he was dead. Yarolala had found her horse, living indeed.

Lightning still stood immobile.

At the first bright shaft of light and the sudden clear carolling of magpies in the sky, Baringa took his mares out of the trees on to Quambat Flat, and he took them towards Cloud, so that they might give ceremonious greeting to the only horse whom he recognised as the leader of Quambat. Baringa, walking proudly at the head of his herd, never even looked at the astonished black stallion, who was further down the flat.

The black stood and stared too. This was not Lightning – the almost beaten Lightning – who walked across the grass, owning the world, and yet bowed so ceremoniously to Cloud as though the world were Cloud's! Was it indeed that bloodstained horse. And the mares! The *white* mares! His own, his very own white mare! He began to gallop. Who was the horse? His hooves thundered on the hollow ground. How many silver horses were there? This time he would *kill*. He, and he alone, the black stallion of the Limestone, would own the world – and those mares!

Cloud saw the black stallion coming, he saw Lightning and Goonda come out of the bush, he heard Baringa finish his gentle greeting, and saw him turn and walk towards the galloping black, walk fast enough to meet the black some distance from his herd.

A sudden shaft of sunlight came down through trees and mountains and lit up Baringa. The black stallion stopped and began to scream and paw the ground. A kurrawong cried wild glory. The eagles appeared in the sky, and Baringa walked on, closer and closer to the black.

The black stopped screaming, stopped pawing the ground, was still for an instant – all gathered together – and sprang!

"He is no fool," Cloud thought. "He wastes no energy on screaming when it really comes to the moment to fight."

The black sprang, but he landed on empty air and came

134

down to the ground on his four hooves with an unexpected crash. Baringa was at one side.

The black stallion swung round and came in more slowly, head snaking, nostrils fiery red, ears flat back – evil. Suddenly something struck him on that snaking head, and Baringa was out of reach again!

Once more the black came snaking forward, even more slowly, as he tried to watch Baringa's movements – but Baringa moved faster than he could imagine. This time a slashing cut on the shoulder steadied the black, and Baringa was standing on his hindlegs in front of him, daring him to come on, daring him to challenge all the strength and power he had gained from his struggles with snow, fire, flood, ice.

This time Baringa let the snaking head almost touch his neck before he crashed both forefeet down. The black stallion was sure he would get his grip that time, and was not prepared to escape. He received three hard blows and gave none.

Next time he rushed at Baringa, Baringa just stood there, shining in the sunshine, then jumped away with a back-lashing kick which got the black on the knee. Sweat streamed in runnels on the black hide, and the smell of his own blood made the black's anger less controllable. He came dashing at Baringa with forelegs striking, flailing, lashing. Baringa stood fast till the last minute, dodging legs, feeling the hot breath, and then suddenly jumped at the attacking horse. Baringa got one slash on the neck, but the black was rocked by the impact and at least one rock-hard blow. Blood began to run into his eye.

The black realised, then, that his wild rushing did no good. He would have to control himself. Fear steadied him down and cooled his anger. Instead of furiously fighting the horse that had his white mare – and the other beautiful mares – he knew he would have to fight a more cunning battle if he were to save himself. Perhaps he could stand back and make the silver horse do the attacking.

He stood still and waited.

Baringa stood too, and while they stood, the eagles floated overhead.

Presently Baringa began to move off towards the black's roan mares. The black went too, but did not attack – not until

135

Baringa started rounding up his mares.

When, at last, a black fury came flying at him through the air, Baringa was ready, and vanished from underneath his feet. Before the black had recovered balance, Baringa was driving his mares off at quite a smart pace.

Then the black seemed to go mad. He galloped after them and hurled himself at Baringa, but there was no possibility of that heavy horse landing on the quick-silver Baringa. Baringa moved just enough to be missed – and, with a tremendously powerful strike which landed on the side of the black's head, knocked him over. Then he started to drive the mares again. The black stallion picked himself up and came galloping alongside Baringa. He made a tremendous spring, sideways, at the silver horse, but it was as though Baringa felt the movement in the air and knew exactly what the other was going to do, because he jumped sideways, lightly and swiftly, snaked his own head forward, and fastened his teeth into the crested black neck.

For a moment Baringa shook him, all his four feet planted firmly, muscles knotting on his great cream neck, chest, shoulders, quarters, then he flung him down, and through this enormous effort, he did not hear the commotion in the watching horses, did not see his grandsire join them like a silver whirlwind.

The black horse regained his balance. Baringa started harrying him, chasing him. They had not gone far when the black sprang on to a rock and defied Baringa. Baringa switched round and mustered up the roan mares again and started to drive them fast towards the lower end of the flat. As soon as they were galloping madly, Baringa stopped and stood still.

The eagles were dropping lower and lower. It was as though they knew that the moment was coming.

Then Baringa attacked.

He rose on his hindlegs and advanced towards the black stallion. He darted first to one side, then to the other: he nipped; he struck; he sprang forward; he sprang back. He went round and round the black, kicking, striking. He sprang up and down in front of him, snaking his head and advancing, feinting to one side and then attacking from the other.

The black was dripping sweat and blood and never touched his opponent. Baringa drove him, yard by yard, down the flat

136

– this horse who had nearly defeated Lightning and whom Lightning could not defeat – slowly exhausting him, because no other horse could keep up with those swift movements.

The roan mares were close, and all the other mares and horses followed some distance behind.

As they were nearing where the trees and the ridges closed in to make the end of the flat, Baringa gave one quick leap forward, grabbed the horse by the wither and hung on. Then he began to shake him, slowly at first, as though he were waiting for something.

Cloud and Thowra and the mares, Lightning and his mares, and the others of Quambat Flat came closer, closer. Overhead the eagles hung in the sky.

Then Baringa braced himself to shake all the strength from the black stallion – shaking, shaking the great black horse.

Before he was badly hurt, Baringa cast him away. The exhausted horse half fell, then struggled up.

"Will you go?" said Baringa, "or must I beat you still further? Do you wish to die?"

The black horse could see his white mare and Dawn and Moon, not far away. He made a great effort to stop his limbs trembling, and launched himself at Baringa, for surely he, the great black stallion of the Limestone, was unbeatable. But Baringa was no longer there. It was only air on which his teeth closed, and something hit him hard on the head again. He turned back dizzily.

He was knocked spinning through space.

It was difficult for him to get up. The ground was rocking.

All the watching horses could see that he was beaten. It looked for a few moments as if he would not be able to raise his head from the ground. Then he forced himself up.

"That is enough," said Baringa sharply, and swung round to look for the roan mares.

The black made one more wild effort to stop him, but Baringa simply bounded forward with a lethal kick of his heels that knocked the black staggering. Then he cantered round those once stolen roans, cut out the two whom Lightning had originally wanted, and sent the rest flying down the track that would take them back to the Limestone.

"Those mares were never won from you by Lightning in
137

fair fight," he said to the shaking, trembling, sweating black, "but if they wish to return, I would not stop them. Now go! And you die, if you ever come back!" Baringa drove the black horse down the creek after his mares.

Just then a great shadow passed over the sunlit grass: it was the eagles flying low. Baringa rose in salute to them. This was the moment which they had all known was coming, the moment even the mares in the Secret Valley had felt to be close in the future, and which had been felt, too, by Baringa's own herd – part of the deep excitement as they waited there in the Canyon for the silver horse descending the cliff.

When he turned round and started to canter back, he saw the grey mares, once owned by Steel, huddled nervously together with the two roans whom he had cut out from the black's five. He checked his pace.

"Don't be afraid," he said to the greys. "Lightning won you from Steel, and I would not take you from my own dam's brother. Go on up the flat, and you too," he said to the roans.

It was then that he saw Thowra. He wanted to greet him, and he wanted to go quickly to Dawn and to all his mares, for the freedom of Quambat Flat and of the southern mountains was now theirs, but first he had to give these mares to Lightning.

He brought the greys and roans right up in front of Lightning and stopped them.

"They are yours," he said to Lightning, and then rubbed his nose on Goonda's and added: "You are all safe here."

He cantered back to his white mares, to his chestnut and his pale blue roan. Dawn came forward to meet him, her foal at her heels.

He greeted his herd and led them up the flat to Cloud. Cloud, while he lived, would always graze at the top of Quambat Flat. Now the old horse rose in salute to the young one who had made this southern land his kingdom, and Baringa rose, too, in graceful greeting, and to his grandsire, who had brought him to Quambat Flat when he was a yearling.

Lightning stood not far away. He had seen all that had taken place, seen Baringa thrash the horse whom he had not been able to beat. Lightning would know for always, now, that Baringa's mares must never be molested, for Baringa –

who had saved him once from Steel, saved him when he was blinded by the fire, and rescued him and his mares when they were hopelessly yarded in the heavy snow – Baringa was an unbeatable fighter, the Silver Stallion of Quambat Flat.

As Baringa and his herd slept that night in moonbar and shade beneath a candlebark, a soft grey shadow hopped through the bush and came quietly beside him, touched his nose with his moon-silvered paw.

Fiction in paperback from Dragon Books

Richard Dubleman
The Adventures of Holly Hobbie   £1.25 ☐

Anne Digby
Trebizon series

First Term at Trebizon   £1.50 ☐
Second Term at Trebizon   £1.50 ☐
Summer Term at Trebizon   £1.50 ☐
Boy Trouble at Trebizon   £1.50 ☐
More Trouble at Trebizon   £1.50 ☐
The Tennis Term at Trebizon   £1.50 ☐
Summer Camp at Trebizon   £1.50 ☐
Into the Fourth at Trebizon   £1.25 ☐
The Hockey Term at Trebizon   £1.50 ☐
The Big Swim of the Summer   60p ☐
A Horse Called September   £1.50 ☐
Me, Jill Robinson and the Television Quiz   £1.25 ☐
Me, Jill Robinson and the Seaside Mystery   £1.25 ☐
Me, Jill Robinson and the Christmas Pantomime   £1.25 ☐
Me, Jill Robinson and the School Camp Adventure   £1.25 ☐

Elyne Mitchell
Silver Brumby's Kingdom   85p ☐
Silver Brumbies of the South   95p ☐
Silver Brumby   85p ☐
Silver Brumby's Daughter   85p ☐
Silver Brumby Whirlwind   50p ☐

Mary O'Hara
My Friend Flicka Part One   85p ☐
My Friend Flicka Part Two   60p ☐

To order direct from the publisher just tick the titles you want
and fill in the order form.

Fiction in paperback from Dragon Books

Peter Glidewell

Schoolgirl Chums	£1.25	☐
St Ursula's in Danger	£1.25	☐
Miss Prosser's Passion	£1.50	☐

Enid Gibson

The Lady at 99	£1.50	☐

Gerald Frow

Young Sherlock: The Mystery of the Manor House	95p	☐
Young Sherlock: The Adventure at Ferryman's Creek	£1.50	☐

Frank Richards

Billy Bunter of Greyfriars School	£1.25	☐
Billy Bunter's Double	£1.25	☐
Billy Bunter Comes for Christmas	£1.25	☐
Billy Bunter Does His Best	£1.25	☐
Billy Bunter's Benefit	£1.50	☐
Billy Bunter's Postal Order	£1.50	☐

Dale Carlson
Jenny Dean Mysteries

Mystery of the Shining Children	£1.50	☐
Mystery of the Hidden Trap	£1.50	☐
Secret of the Third Eye	£1.50	☐

Marlene Fanta Shyer

My Brother the Thief	95p	☐

David Rees

The Exeter Blitz	£1.50	☐

Caroline Akrill

Eventer's Dream	£1.50	☐
A Hoof in the Door	£1.50	☐
Ticket to Ride	£1.50	☐

Michel Parry (ed)

Superheroes	£1.25	☐

Ulick O'Connor

Irish Tales and Sagas	£2.95	☐

To order direct from the publisher just tick the titles you want
and fill in the order form.

Fiction in paperback from Dragon Books

Mr T   £1.50 ☐

Ann Jungman
Vlad the Drac   £1.25 ☐
Vlad the Drac Returns   £1.25 ☐
Vlad the Drac Superstar   £1.50 ☐

Jane Holiday
Gruesome and Bloodsocks   £1.25 ☐

Thomas Meehan
Annie   £1.50 ☐

Michael Denton
Eggbox Brontosaurus   £1.25 ☐
Glitter City   £1.25 ☐
Fantastic   £1.25 ☐

Marika Hanbury Tenison
The Princess and the Unicorn   £1.25 ☐

Alan Davidson
A Friend Like Annabel   £1.25 ☐
Just Like Annabel   £1.25 ☐

Maureen Spurgeon
BMX Bikers   £1.50 ☐
BMX Bikers and the Dirt-Track Racers   £1.50 ☐

T R Burch
Ben and Blackbeard   £1.25 ☐
Ben on Cole's Hill   £1.25 ☐

Jonathan Rumbold
The Adventures of Niko   £1.25 ☐

Marcus Crouch
The Ivory City   95p ☐

Lynne Reid Banks
The Indian in the Cupboard   £1.50 ☐

Nina Beachcroft
A Spell of Sleep   £1.25 ☐
Cold Christmas   £1.50 ☐

Graham Marks
The Finding of Stoby Binder   £1.50 ☐

David Osborn
Jessica and the Crocodile Knight   £1.50 ☐

To order direct from the publisher just tick the titles you want
and fill in the order form.

All these books are available at your local bookshop or newsagent, or can be ordered direct from the publisher.

To order direct from the publishers just tick the titles you want and fill in the form below.

Name _____

Address _____

Send to:
Dragon Cash Sales
PO Box 11, Falmouth, Cornwall TR10 9EN.

Please enclose remittance to the value of the cover price plus:

UK 45p for the first book, 20p for the second book plus 14p per copy for each additional book ordered to a maximum charge of £1.63.

BFPO and Eire 45p for the first book, 20p for the second book plus 14p per copy for the next 7 books, thereafter 8p per book.

Overseas 75p for the first book and 21p for each additional book.

Dragon Books reserve the right to show new retail prices on covers, which may differ from those previously advertised in the text or elsewhere.